Stories

Sunil Gangopadhyay

translated by
Sheila Sengupta

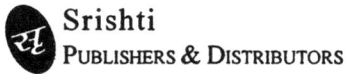
Srishti
PUBLISHERS & DISTRIBUTORS

Srishti Publishers & Distributors
Registered Office: N-16, C.R. Park
New Delhi – 110 019
Corporate Office: 212A, Peacock Lane
Shahpur Jat, New Delhi – 110 049
editorial@srishtipublishers.com

First English translation published by Srishti Publishers & Distributors in 2006

Copyright © original Bangla with Sunil Gangopadhyay
Copyright © English translation with Sheila Sengupta

ISBN 81-88575-83-6

Typeset in AGaramond 11pt. by Suresh Kumar Sharma at Srishti

Cover design: Sandip Sinha

All rights reserved. No part of this publication may be reproduced, stored in a retrieval system, or transmitted, in any form or by any means, electronic, mechanical, photocopying, recording or otherwise, without the prior written permission of the Publishers.

Contents

	Introduction	vii
	Translator's note	xiii
1.	A fugitive and a follower *Palatak O Anusarankari*	1
2.	Skyscraper *Akashchumbi*	15
3.	Riverside *Naditeere*	23
4.	The wooden bridge *Sanko*	35
5.	Virtue and sin *Dharmadhormo*	49
6.	Our Manorama *Amader Manorama*	69
7.	Shajehan and his own battalion *Shahjahan O tar Nijashwa Bahini*	103
8.	Damayanti's face *Damayantir Mukh*	125
9.	A cup of tea at the Taj Mahal *Taj Mahale ek Cup Cha*	149
10.	Blood and tears *Rakta ebong Asru*	171

Introduction

Sunil Gangopadhyay (born 1934 in Faridpur, now in Bangladesh), the Bengali novelist, poet and short story writer, winner of, amongst others, the Sahitya Akademi Award in 1985, India's most prestigious literary award, is one of India's leading writers today, a voice that is noted for its fearless radicalism, wit, realism and humanism. This collection of ten short stories, translated with sensitive proximity to the original by Sheila Sen Gupta, is an eclectic selection of his modern fiction. Set mostly in contemporary times, they could happen in any period anywhere in the world, such is the universality of the characters' experiences and events. Yet they succeed in encapsulating India's long history, conveying the contradictions that make up the vibrant fabric of India.

Every story comes as a surprise, each different from the others, the characters brought sharply alive as they unfold through the dialogues that are so much in character and fit the descriptions of them. The age-old dilemma of religious conflict, which can ignite into a conflagration in India's volatile communal politics, is captured in the curious confrontation of police bureaucracy caught in the web of popular beliefs and concerns one rainy night in 'Virtue and Sin'. The presiding Police Inspector Rahman suddenly sees the clouds on his consciousness lifting as the new moon appears and fills him with the pride of finding and guarding a valuable Hindu idol.

The communal dilemma acquires a complex twist in the long short story of the Dalit Bangshi, the village idiot who has the uncanny talent of appearing at the heart of chaos to become the target of inhuman beatings whenever the crowd needs a victim to chastise, reflecting the peculiar mentality of mob violence which targets the defenceless. Ironically, the story is entitled 'Blood and Tears' and though Bangshi is beaten time and again till he bleeds, he is unable to shed tears to the consternation of his torturers. Bangshi is a sculptor in whose hands clay speaks eloquently, leaving his spectators jealously hostile. He has learnt the art from a Muslim mentor whose hands are cut off by his co-religionists for over-stepping, in their opinion, socio-religious boundaries. The conflicts of religious beliefs, superstitions and interests, threaten to paralyse Bangshi in a similar way, till, by a strange chain of events, he is sought out by the same judgemental society that once set out to nearly cripple him, to give shape to the deity he has emotionally and artistically striven towards all his artistic life.

There is a touch of mystery in many of Gangopadhyay's stories, which makes them exciting reading, sometimes leaving the reader with innumerable questions, the ends untied, with many 'maybes …' adding to their charm. Manorama, the eponymous heroine of the story which bears her name, has all the unheroine-like qualities of being hefty, having a booming voice, ungainly hips and breasts, and is of a dark complexion, with a pock-marked face, yet she musters the joint devotion of four workers who consider themselves her self-appointed guardians and are her secret and jealous admirers. There is the undiluted pleasure of the Saturday dance and a platonic game of suggestive pleasure that this harmless quartet plays with Manorama, which is suddenly interrupted by the unprecedented. Gangopadhyay's wry humour is evident in the metaphoric reading of the precarious existence of these men in their work as workers of a matchstick company, that brittle tool that has a short existence, its slender reality open to speculation about its continuity in the face of more stout competition in a fast changing economy. And the threat comes in the shape of a stranger, gentlemanly in appearance, who turns up one night and cannot be moved because of his burning fever. Who is this stranger? Where has he come from and why has he come here? How long will he stay? As Manorama feels she has to nurse him, her devoted troupe is harried with these unasked questions, just as the reader is, unravelling the skein of human longing for security, freedom or romance.

The stranger could be a political activist on the run, a Naxalite fleeing detection from the police or running away from his opponents as in 'The Fugitive and Follower'. The unexpected gives a juicy twist to the tale as the fugitive is first pursued by the followers who chase their game, tenaciously following a 'list' of possibilities. Once the 'fugitive' is killed, his three 'followers' then become the hounded as nine pursuers divide up in separate teams of three, the chase beginning again, with similar lists giving the cue for possible escape routes of the would-be victim. In another story of pursuit, 'The Bridge,' we encounter the experience of a knife-edge situation as sadistic pursuers play a cat and mouse game with a prisoner who is made to walk a tight rope in a dance of the macabre. Just as he reaches the end, while the waters of the fierce Teesta gush below in the depths of the gorge on a dark moonless night, the fugitive starts walking back, leaving his captors breathless with amazement and uncertainty. The reader can hang narrowly on to hope in stories like this, visualising possibilities of tables turning here as in 'The Fugitive and the Follower'.

The theme of escape finds fresh expression in the story of the reclusive life of Archishman waking up everyday to the stunning beauty of the Himalayas in 'Damayanti's Face'. The charisma of the simple, self-effacing 'Yogibaba' seems to reflect the humbling, unspoilt wonder of the range that surrounds them. Layers of mountain mists lift as we realise that the hermit, in his wish to escape, has actually sought refuge from the agony of missing his chance of a romantic attachment to the girl he has always loved. But the mountains do not shut him in or the face of the woman he loved, out, and Archishman dies, watched over by the face of Damayanti, the woman he has tried to forget and remained faithful to in his hermit's existence. This cinematic framing of the recluse's past life etches him out as painfully human, having all the failings of selfish ownership that the best of people find themselves guilty of.

Time and again, Gangopadhyay's protagonists are the poorest of the poor, the ordinary man, the farm labourer or urban worker, depicted with his irrepressible humour in incongruous yet probable situations. 'Tea at the Taj Mahal' is a refreshing comedy, verging on the ridiculous, defiantly challenging the democratic claims of the Indian constitution as one popularly claimed leader of the people, the 'Ustadji,' leads a procession of riffraffs from their village fields in Hamlyn-style to the capital, hitch-hiking truck rides and appearing at the gates of the five star hotel. The theatre of the Absurd unfolds as the hotel staff end up serving tea to this ragged group, poured out by the one-day 'Begum' in the tearfully grateful Phoolsaria. This is the most unlikely tea party to have occurred in a free India. There is a Narayanesque sensitivity and humour in stories like this and 'Shahjehan and his own battalion'. In the latter, the village idiot, like Bangshi of 'Blood and Tears', has the knack of ending up as the victim of every calamity and skirmish. He is only capable of sitting and staring into space, but suddenly discovers the royal significance of his name as he can order and control into action, direct and motivate a colony of ants on the wall in the bathroom where he is happy to stand and stare all day!

The urban workers' lives are painted with tender romance in a dreamlike sequence as a couple move up the flight of stairs in a tower block in 'The Skyscraper', and choose a room to spend the night in, flinging their dreams across the balconies. For the moment, they can dream in this very building they have built for the fulfilment of the dreams of rich families, before ownership begins the next day and they have to make way for those they serve.

Just as Gangopadhyay can give identities and expression to the fugitive and follower, the rural labourer and urban worker, the Muslim Police Inspector, the Hindu thief, the prostitute and the tea-stall woman owner, he can portray the sense of isolation and the need to search for solace and self-identity through a metaphoric dialogue with the Prime Minister of India, Indira Gandhi in 'Riverside'. The image of a plane ride, the struggle between the public and private spheres in a political cult-like figure like Indira Gandhi, capture the hectic speed of activity and the near-impossibility of escaping the clicking flashes of recognition in countless cameras and the probing, watchful eyes of the media and a whole population. Yet, just as the river

Hoogly flows through time, symbolising the sacredness of rivers and life in India, people have held onto this desire to stand on the brink of this inevitable stream of continuity and amidst its variable waters, to be with oneself, confronting one's own heart and soul, watched by a rising, or, as in this case, a setting sun. This is a moving story of India's iron woman, seeking the solitude of the riverside, encouraged and aided to walking incognito for a special moment of confessional solitude. The point about bodyguards and their ubiquitous presence is made in multiple references, a fact that the world will have in mind in any story of Indira Gandhi, which is so poignantly stressed in this story while much is left unsaid. And this is what marks Sunil Gangopadhyay's short stories, their tender humanism, their refreshing humour and the unsaid, that ability to leave something for the reader to decipher, weave, create, in a shared understanding of the unspoken, which is the hallmark of a master craftsman of the short story.

Dr Bashabi Fraser
Honorary Fellow,
Centre for South Asian Studies,
Edinburgh University

A few words from the Translator

Among the contemporary Bengali literary personalities, Sunil Gangopadhyay is a leading and extremely popular writer, his popularity having remained unchanged for almost four decades now. Even though he started first by writing poetry, Gangopadhyay soon made his literary presence felt in the world of prose, and since then, has made invaluable contribution in almost every field of Bengali literature. Unlike his novels, most of which have been translated either into English or some other Indian language, his innumerable short stories have been translated rather sporadically, and therefore it was felt that a select collection of his stories, translated into English would be a welcome addition to the world of translations.

The stories in this book have been selected by the author himself and even though they are varied in their tone and content, a subtle continuity can be felt as the stories unfold. To quote the author's own words "In my own life and the life that I see around me, there is so much to write about, but not all of that can be expressed in words. The main difficulty lies in deciding where to start the story from. Sometimes even a sudden word or a scene can spark off an idea and a story gradually built around it."

The stories in this volume, even though told very simply, leave a mark in the novelty of their content and presentation. And each of them carries the hallmark of the author's very own literary style. Whether it's the story surrounding the ungainly Manorama, the good – for nothing Haju, the poor but talented sculptor Bangshi, all of them reveal the ease with which

Gangopadhyay weaves remarkable stories around simple people and their simple lives, that touch the reader's heart.

Given my own limitations, it has not been easy to maintain the same lucidity in language and expression, even as I tried to remain faithful to the original. However, I sincerely hope that the translations will at least help readers, outside Bengal, to get a glimpse into the writings of one of the leading contemporary writers of our times.

I would like to thank the author for his help and words of encouragement throughout this work. A very special acknowledgment to Dr. Bashabi Fraser, of Edinburgh University for writing a very comprehensive and detailed introduction to the book, and to Srishti Publishers, Delhi for bringing out this volume. I remain indebted to all of them for helping give shape to an idea that was born a long time ago.

Sheila Sengupta
New Delhi
December, 2005

A Fugitive and a Follower
Palatak O Anusarankari

"You?"

"Shh ..." Robi whispered, putting a finger on his lips. Then with a swift glance over his shoulder, he took a step forward and asked "Is Uncle at home? Is Asutosh there?"

"No. they're not at home." Jayanti said, shaking her head.

"Is *Pishima* there?"

"Yes." Jayanti replied, then eyeing him cursorily, said – "There's such a lot of mud on your feet! Go and wash it off."

She followed him to the courtyard, and opened the tap in the corner "Where have you been for so long?" she asked lowering her voice.

"*Boudi*, I am very hungry. Do you have something to eat? Even *muri* will do." Robi said, evading her question.

"Come upstairs with me."

The stairs led to the first floor. Robi saw *Pishima* standing on the landing. The old woman's sight had been failing with age. Straining her eyes to have a better look, she asked, "Who is it, *Bouma?*"

"Oh, its our Robi."

The faded eyes turned towards Robi. The child had grown into a young man, but those eyes still saw the child in him.

"Come closer! Why are you still standing there?" she said.

"*Pishima*, I am very hungry."

The old woman seemed to expect a *pranam*, but did a hungry man ever remember such niceties? Turning to Jayanti, Robi said, "Boudi, could you please hurry up."

"Will you be leaving just now? Aren't you going to stay back tonight?" Pishima asked.

"Let Ashok*da* come. I have something to tell him."

"How is *Barda?*"

"He's just the same."

"And your mother? It's so long since I heard from her."

Robi could feel a spurt of anger, "Didn't I say I was hungry?" He said sternly. "Are you going to give me something to eat or do you want to go on cross-examining me?"

– "Oh my, what temper! How long is it since you ate last?"

At this moment, Jayanti returned, carrying a tasty looking dish of *muri* mixed with minced onions, chillies and *chanachur*. Handing it to Robi, she said – "Eat this for the time being. I'll just go and fry some *luchis*..."

"No, this will do. You don't have to make *luchis* now."

"Shall I make some tea?"

"Yes, you may."

"Robi, you have thinned down so much in just a month's time. Don't you have any concern for yourself?" Jayanti asked.

"And what about Ashokda? He has been putting on so much weight by the day. Can't you look after your husband's health?"

"Your eyes look completely sunken. How many nights have you not slept?"

"Go and put the water to boil." Robi retorted, ignoring her remark. Then munching some muri, he came and stood by the window. It had grown dark outside. Narrowing his eyes a little, Robi looked around cautiously.

After a while, he saw three men coming towards this house. They seemed completely engrossed talking to each other. On coming closer, they looked up and stood motionless for a moment. Then, as if heaving a long sigh in unison, they resumed their walk, coming closer to the house.

In a quick move, Robi set aside his plate and ran out of the room. Without bidding farewell to any member of the family he ran down the stairs, and once outside the house, he started running frantically.

On reaching the house, the three men looked around, and for a moment saw Robi's disappearing form in the distance. But they did not show any urgency or hurriedness in their move.

Follower number 1 said, "He has again escaped us this time."

Follower number 2 said, "Doesn't matter."

Taking out a piece of paper from his pocket, follower number

3 tried to read the scribble on it. "What's the next destination?" He asked. "Dum Dum or Srirampur?"

Number 2 said, "Lets' finish our part of the business here."

Shoving his hands into his coat pocket, number 3 said, 'Its getting pretty cold tonight. Guess what? While we were coming here, I saw some sizzling cutlets being sold in the restaurant at the corner."

Taking out a bomb from the bag strung on his shoulder, number 1 hurled it toward the house, targetting the door. A loud explosion seared through the silent night.

"Good, that sounded well. "Number 2 said in a satisfied way.

"There's no need to hurry." Number 3 said. "Come, let's go and have some cutlets in that hotel."

Standing in front of another house, Robi lowered his voice and called out, "Chandan, Chandan!"

There was no answer. It was almost half past nine in the evening. The suburban town seemed totally desolate. The stillness around was broken at times only by a rickshaw-horn or the irrelevant bark of a stray dog.

"Chandan," Robi called out louder this time.

A young girl leaned over from the verandah on the first floor. "Who is it?" she asked.

"Is Chandan at home?"

"Dada is not well."

"Can't he get up from the bed?"

"He is sleeping."

"Just open the door once."

"What's your name?"

"Open the door, first."

With a swift movement, Robi glanced over his head. Two rickshaws had just stopped on the main road. Robi couldn't afford to wait for the door to open. He ran and vanished into the darkness.

The three men came and stood in front of the house. Number 1 said, "I could make out quite clearly that he didn't go in."

Without another word, he walked towards the door. Even before he could push against it, the door opened. A young girl, about fourteen or fifteen years old, stood in the doorway. She was clad in a sari but from the way she wore it, it was obvious that she had just started wearing them.

"Is Chandan really sick?" Number 2 asked, his voice sounding calm.

"Yes, he has a temperature of about a hundred and four degrees now. Where are you all from?"

"From Robi Babu. May we see your brother for a minute?"

"He's sleeping."

"Alright then."

"Would you like to leave a message for him?"

"Tell him that three men had come here in search of Robi Babu. That'll be enough for him to understand."

As soon as Number 2 moved away from the door, Number 3 said, "Do we need to use *that* here?"

Number 1 said, "I think ..."

Number 3 said, "My younger brother too has not been keeping well. I feel I will also fall ill very soon."

No 2 placed a hand on his forehead, and said – "But, you don't seem to have any temperature at all."

"I am feeling feverish inside ... Oh if I could only curl up under a blanket now."

"Let us finish our job here." Number 1 said. " There's no use in delaying any further."

Number 3 said, "I've not had a wink of sleep for quite some time now. And its so cold today. God doesn't seem to have any mercy on us."

Number 2 said, "This son of a ... is really giving us a lot of trouble."

Number 1 fished out a bomb from his shoulder bag and hurled it at the door. A deafening noise pierced through the silence of the winter night. The street dogs in the distance wailed aloud.

Robi spent the entire night sitting on the cremation ground by the side of the Ganga. Whenever he felt he was going to doze off, he stood up quickly and took a walk. At times he went and stood by a funeral pyre. Four pyres kept burning throughout the night. There was no end to people coming and going from the burning ghat. No one asked him anything. The smoke from the pyres went into his eyes, so with tears streaming down, he could easily pass off as one of the pall bearers or mourners.

It was indeed a long time since Robi had shed tears at anybody's death. While standing in the crematorium, one realized even more that death was only a matter of total detachment and that there was nothing good or bad about it. Robi touched his bare chest. He felt a sudden desire to caress himself. He kept moving his hand fondly over his own chest imagining it to be that of someone else.

Then, as dawn broke out, he mingled with those who had come to take a dip in the Ganges and walked back with them to the Howrah Station. From there, he boarded a train to Srirampur.

Sushanto was about to leave for the market, his bag all ready in hand, when Robi reached his house.

"I am going to stay here tonight." Robi announced.

Sushanto hesitated for a moment. "My father is coming here from Delhi today." He said.

"But I have to stay here at least for one day." Robi said.

"Khokan is at Gonsai Para. Shall I send for him?"

"No, that won't be necessary."

Robi spent the entire night sleeping soundly, a sleep that was long overdue. He awoke only once to take bath and have his food. He spent a long time in the bath, but it didn't take him long to finish his food. His clothes had become so dirty that it would not be proper to change into them after his bath. So he had to wear Sushanto's *dhoti* and *kurta*. He was looking quite different now. As sleep began to overtake him, he muttered, slowly to himself, "If only I could change into a different person now, the same way as I could change my clothes. If only ..."

Robi fell asleep again. In his sleep, he dreamt of a ship.

When he woke up, it had grown dark outside. The twilight had deepened to a deep blue. Stepping out of the small attic on the terrace where he had been given shelter, he looked around. No, there was nobody in sight.

After a while, Sushanto's wife Rupa brought him a cup of tea. Taking a sip, Robi asked, "Do you have an aspirin or something?"

"No I don't. Shall I get you some from the dispensary?"

"No, it doesn't matter. The headache has been bothering me for quite some time now. I get it every evening and it goes on its own. Isn't Sushanto back from work yet?"

"He will be, soon."

"You may go downstairs now but send Sushanto when he comes home."

"Would you like to eat something?"

"Nobody has ever coaxed me to eat. I'll let you know when I am hungry. Do you have any *Moong Dal* at home? Will you be able to prepare it tonight? It's so long since I tasted it."

"Why, didn't you ...?"

"Please leave now. I want to be by myself for a while."

Without switching on the lights Robi kept sitting in the dark, staring grimly at the white walls. He continued to stare in front of him without shifting his gaze even once. After some time, he sat up a little and clutched at the vein throbbing on his forehead.

"Why have you not switched the light on?" Sushanto asked as he stepped into the room, a few minutes later.

"I have heard a dog barking for quite some time now." Robi said. "You know, I used to have a dog when I was a child, and it had a very similar bark. It was just like this."

"Where is that dog now?"

"We used to live in Shiv Sagar then. The dog used to be with me all the time. It was a very gentle and docile dog. But suddenly one day, God knows why, it became very angry and rough. It started frightening everybody. My parents said that it had gone mad. I didn't agree with them but they didn't dare to keep it in the house any more. One day, they coaxed it to leave the house with them and carried it in a ship to the other side of the river. They left it there on high land. And that land often got flooded. From that time, whenever I hear a dog bark in some desolate place ..."

"Where will you be going from here?"

"I don't know."

"You can stay here for a day or two. This room is not used anyway."

Robi stared at Sushanto. Then with a sudden note of conceit in his voice he said, "Even if I don't have a roof over my head, it doesn't matter. I didn't exactly have a room in mind when I had stepped out on the road."

"Robi, we have to change our direction now." Sushanto said, sternly. "The path that you are following is not a proper one. It's only a narrow lane."

"I say Sushanto, you must be having a gramophone in this house, isnt it?"

"Why do you ask this, suddenly?"

"Oh everybody knows, a gramophone in the corner always symbolises a happy, contented household. Without that it doesn't look nice."

"This is just false conceit on your part."

At that moment Rupa came hurriedly into the room. "Three men have come to call you." She told Sushanto, in a tone of urgency.

Robi sprang up immediately and ran towards the terrace. Peeping cautiously, he looked over his shoulders. "Is there a door at the back?" he asked in a calm voice.

Sushanto held on to his hands desperately, and whispered, "Are you leaving now?"

"I don't have any option."

"Robi you don't have to go. There is nothing to be so afraid of. I'll go and talk to those people downstairs."

"Its not fear, Sushanto, its hatred. Anyway, I really don't have any more time."

"Why are you behaving in such a strange manner? There's a telephone next door. I can inform the police."

Without glancing at Rupa even once, Robi ran towards the parapet, and jumped over it to climb down the water pipe at the back. Somewhere in the distance, a train passed by noisily.

Follower number 1 said, "See, these houses are numbered so haphazardly! House number 52 is next to house number 37. This is really terrible!"

Follower number 2 said, "And some houses are not even numbered."

Number 1 said, "Last year at about this time, I was on the run. That had been really more thrilling."

Number 2 said, "The day Bardhan died ..."

Number 3 said, "You know there is a guava tree in my grandparents' house, the fruits are red inside. I had fallen off that tree once as a little child. Since then, one of my legs has become rather weak."

"You said the guava was red inside!" Number 2 exclaimed.

Number 1 said, "Such guavas are available in Deoghar also. I had gone there once with my elder brother and his wife."

Number 2 said, "Come on, let us finish our job here."

Number 3 said, "After that we can all go and get some sound sleep. Just imagine – a meal of freshly prepared rice and dal served hot, boiled potatoes ..."

Number 1 turned to the door to talk to Sushanto. The other two men moved to the two sides of the house.

Robi was running desperately. He stopped for a moment, and asked a stranger passing by, "Can you tell me the way to the station?"

"Why are you going through this dark field? Take the road over there ..."

"Can't I go through the field?"

"You can, but you may not be able to find your way."

"I will. Just show me." Robi replied, in a tone that sounded almost like a snub.

Unperturbed at the rough tone, the man said, "Well, since you insist on going through the field, you might as well find your own way."

Robi threw an angry look at the man and continued running. He was taking measured breaths now. Obviously, he couldn't afford to tire himself out. He was alone, but a thousand breaths seemed to mingle in the surrounding air. Even breaths of these who were long dead!

Looking over his head from time to time, Robi continued to run. Beads of perspiration shone on his skin even on that cold winter night. Suddenly, he hit a wall.

It wasn't a wall. They were three men. Gripping him with trained hands, they stopped him abruptly. Robi didn't move, he just covered his face with both hands.

Removing his hands from his face forcibly, Number 1 said "Robi can you recognize me?"

Number 2 said, "Remember, the three of you had attacked Bardhanda?"

Number 3 said, "Scoundrel, you have given us enough trouble ..."

Robi didn't say a word. Suddenly, he remembered he was to have sent a box of coloured pencils to his little sister. She had requested Robi twice or thrice already.

A dagger shone through the darkness. In a silent move, the three men plunged it into Robi's chest and stomach, again and again, almost cutting his body into pieces. They waited a few more minutes to assure themselves that he had stopped breathing.

Around this time, some voices were heard in the distance. About eight or ten people were seen running this way.

The three men turned around and saw them. They felt puzzled. Were those people coming to congratulate them or arrest them? In either case, the accompanying cries generally sounded similar. The three men didn't take any chance. Without another word they stood up and started running, in three different directions, to avoid being caught. Almost at once, the large crowd arrived on the spot. They glanced at Robi's motionless body only once and then took a solemn pledge.

There were nine men in this group. They divided themselves into three groups and started running in three different directions. The one who was follower number 1 till now was now fugitive number 1. The new follower number 1 asked his fellow members, "Where can he escape? Take out that slip of paper from your pocket. Read it."

Skyscraper
Akashchumbi

It had been raining since the evening. Not very hard – just a drizzle. There was no electricity in this city for quite some time now, but that didn't really matter. There was no difference between the streets of Calcutta and a village in the darkness. In any case, the young couple did not find it difficult to walk in the dark.

Leaving behind the Gariahat crossing, they walked on towards Golpark. There was a crowd of people all around, but the two of them seemed to be in a world of their own. They moved on- engrossed only in themselves.

The girl was wearing a sari with a floral print. Her name was Munni. The boy wore a blue shirt over a pleated dhoti. His name was Jadu. Both of them looked lean, with no extra flab anywhere. Only some parts of their bodies were smeared with dust.

Suddenly, Munni said, "Lets' have rice tonight."

"Why, won't you eat *rotis?* That shop doesn't serve rice." Jadu told her.

"Lets' eat at some other place today. I don't feel like having *rotis* tonight." Munni said, and then with a sudden smile added, "I'll pay for the food today."

On one side of the Lakes located in the Southern Avenue, there stood a row of shops with a hotel somewhere in the middle. Every night Jadu and Munni had dinner at this hotel. Roti, rice-dal, vegetables, egg curry, and mince meat curry was what they would generally order. Freshly made chapattis were served hot, and with that, onions and chillies as much as one wanted.

There was also a Chinese restaurant across the road, but it didn't attract as large a crowd as this restaurant did. Tonight, Munni and Jadu didn't go there. Crossing the Dhakuria Bridge, they came and stood in front of a hotel behind the bus depot.

Inside the hotel, a lone *hazak* burnt in the dark. A few benches were laid here and there. The air around was filled with the aroma of *dal* made with freshly chopped onions.

Munni and Jadu hesitated a little before walking in.

A young waiter stepped outside and greeted them, "Come in, come in, there's place here."

The two of them looked at each other and laughed aloud, for no particular reason.

As starters for dinner, they chose rice, *dal, and bhindi*. Even before they could finish that, the young bearer raised his voice and announced, "What more would you like to have? *Parshey* fish, *Tangra* fish, mutton curry, fowl curry ..."

Munni said, "Ill have meat today."

Jadu had nothing against that. Both of them were carrying a lot of money. They ordered a plate of mutton with gravy and some more rice.

This rice bought from the city was of fine grain and didn't seem to meet their approval.

Munni, still lingering on her chair, demanded, "We'll have *paan* now."

Jadu bought four *paans* from the *Paan* shop. The *paans* were made of sweet betel leaves, flavoured with areca-nut, *jarda* and cloves. He held out a five rupee note to the panwallah, quite unhesitatingly.

The two of them then walked down the road aimlessly. All of a sudden it started raining again, and they ran to take shelter under a balcony nearby. It was now time to go home.

Actually, one could do without an umbrella in this city. From the shelter of one balcony to another, and at times taking refuge under the sheds of the roadside shops, one could easily keep on moving without getting drenched.

So, they walked on until they reached a house – a huge building really. A number of people lay huddled on the ground floor, possibly lulled to sleep by the cool showers. Together, the two of them climbed up to the first floor.

"Lets' go up further." Munni demanded.

It was a brand new, shining white house. The walls had been painted just yesterday. The smell of fresh paint still lingered in the air. In fact the paint on the window grills was still quite wet. It could easily stain their hands if they touched it now.

The doors were being fitted in the door-frames from today, the rooms were not closed yet.

"I want to go further up." Munni repeated

"What's the point of going further? Jadu asked "Will you be staying back here tonight?"

"No, no, let's just keep climbing higher."

Putting an arm round her lovingly, Jadu said "Oh my, just see, you've got completely drenched!"

"As if you haven't!" Munni said laughing aloud.

Jadu took off his shirt and then looked at Munni. Obviously Munni couldn't take off her saree. She would change it later. Right now, she was completely enchanted with the idea of climbing up.

After reaching the sixth floor, Jadu said, "I am feeling exhausted now. We don't have to go up any further. See how beautiful this room is. There's a window on every wall."

Munni stepped inside and inspected the room carefully. It was quite dark of course, but still, a faint glow of light reflected from the freshly painted white walls. She walked out onto the long adjoining balcony and looked around. It was really amusing to see the tall coconut trees so far below. During her days back in the village, she had seen these trees stand higher than even the tallest of the houses in her neighbourhood. And now ...

Opening her mouth a little, Munni spat out a blob. Within seconds, that little blob of spit vanished in the air. Then, turning around, she again said, "Come, lets' go up."

"Again? Didn't you like this room?" Jadu asked.

Laughing merrily, Munning kept swaying her head this way

and that. There were so many rooms in this building. Maybe a hundred, or two hundred, and she could stay in any one of those! Even the emperors didn't have so many rooms, did they!

"Come on, lets' go please, come." She coaxed.

Seventh floor, eighth floor, ninth ... By the time she reached the tenth floor her legs started aching. Holding onto the staircase railings, she began to take long gasps of breath.

Jadu wasn't going to stop here. When they had come up so high, why shouldn't they climb up right to the top of the building?"

Tugging at her hand Jadu said "Come on."

"Wait, I am out of breath!"

In a flash of a second, Jadu swept Munni off her feet and straight into his arms. Flaying her arms and legs frantically, Munni protested. "What's this? leave me, let me go please. See, I'm about to fall, and you're tired too!"

But did anyone really listen to her cries! Holding Munni in his arms, Jadu started climbing up the steps, as fast as he could.

On reaching the top, he put her down by the wall, in just the same way as he would rest a rolled-up mat. He was also beginning to feel tired now. His chest was heaving.

Eleventh floor. This was the highest. There were no lights in the entire building, but a faint glow from the night sky lit this floor. The outlines of Munni's body were clearly visible as the wet sari clung to her.

'We're going to stay here' Jadu said. "Above everyone's head. You can select the room you would like to sleep in."

There were so many rooms here, one after another. Any of

those could serve as their bedroom tonight. From this height, the entire city seemed below their feet. The distant horizon seemed like an endless ocean.

Jadu kept moving his hands against the walls slowly, with affection. He remembered how Munni had carried the bricks on her head, and he had cemented each of these walls. This room was his creation. Rather it was their's.

From tomorrow, the rooms would be fitted with doors, and the doors with locks. Then they would all be closed.

From tomorrow, the electrician and plumber would start their work. Jadu and Munni's share of work was over. They would have to leave.

Till tonight, both of them had full right over these rooms. They were going to lie next to each other and spend the night in the best room of this city, the room that they had built with their own hands. They would not sleep, they were going to spend the night just talking to each other.

Both of them were now moving their hands lovingly on the walls, praising its smoothness.

"Aren't you going to take off that drenched saree now?" Jadu asked. "After all, there's no one here. What's there to feel shy about?"

"No, I will not take it off." Munni replied, crossing her eyebrows in an enchanting manner."

They came and stood in the verandah. Like any other young couple of the city, they put their arms around each other. Their cheeks touched.

"Our home-this is our home." Munni said, laughingly.

Pulling her even closer, Jadu repeated "Yes, our home."

And then both of them laughed out in a frenzied manner.

After a while Munni leaned over the verandah and put out her tongue.

In the darkness below, the city lay asleep. Munni turned her face and looked up.

"What are you doing" Jadu asked.

"Look, look, the sky has come so close." Munni said "We can easily stretch out our hands and touch it. Isn't it?"

Jadu reached out, "Why, but I can't feel it."

"Oh you stupid man! You don't understand anything." Munni said.

"See, the clouds are coming down. Its' going to rain very soon. Why don't you taste the clouds a bit? I can feel them on my tongue."

Jadu put his tongue out also.

And then both of them kept tasting the clouds in sheer delight.

Riverside
Naditeere

And then, I asked Indira Gandhi "Do you like to read books?"

With a faint smile on her lips, Mrs Gandhi replied, "You know as a child I was a book worm."

"But, now you possibly don't get much time to read, do you?"

"No I don't. But then, whenever I can save a little time as when travelling from one place to another – which I often need to do, I generally don't talk to anybody, just read. I remember once on my way to Assam I had taken with me Andre Malreaux's "Anti Memoires", of which I could read only forty-eight pages. I left it with a page mark. After that I didn't get an opportunity on that trip. Later, on a trip to Luxembourg I started again from the forty ninth page."

"That book has some wonderful things about your father."

"Yes."

I stopped talking and picked up a scented tissue from my

side. Such tissues are served on all flights, a moist piece of soft paper which can be used for cleansing one's face while its sweet scent also cheers the heart. When the airhostess had brought these napkins on a tray, I had picked up three instead of one. This is generally not done but no one minds if one breaks the rule.

I wondered whether Mrs Gandhi ever did the same, that is – picked up three napkins instead of one. But then it dawned on me that perhaps she never needed to. She was never confronted with such situations.

Mrs.Gandhi changed her posture by crossing one leg over the other. She flattened the folds of her saree draped around her thighs, lifted up her chin in a child-like manner and drifted into a thoughtful silence.

After a while, with a distracted look in her eyes she said, "You know people come to me with so many different queries. But I never ask anyone about anything. My task is to only answer them."

"And, I presume these are mostly inconsequential queries?"

"Almost."

"I have just one more question to ask. How do you find this life of yours? Is this what you would call 'bliss'?"

"Bliss?"

"Yes."

"Oh I have never thought of bliss. All through my life, whenever I have been confronted with any kind of a difficult situation, I have only hoped that nobody should be able to defeat me! After all I have never lost! A lot might have remained incomplete, but I have never lost."

"Maybe you have not read Rabindranth's "*Gandhari'r Abedon*". In that book he has expressed the same thoughts through Duryadhan's speech:

I don't want bliss, oh Lord

Victory! I had wanted victory, today I am victorious!

Small joys cannot fill the heart of a Kshatriya.

"You are comparing me to *Duryadhan*?"

"Now you are the one who is asking a question!"

"No this is a counter question, meant only to simplify the answer itself."

"No I didn't make any comparisons. One cannot compare life with a novel. In any case, the character of *Duryodhan* depicted in the *Mahabharata* and the one created by Rabindranath are not the same. All that I was trying to say was that, those in charge of governance, always hold victory as their main objective. In the *dharma* of kings, there is no place for fellow feeling or friendship, its only the *dharma* of victory.

"Actually, I had made that remark only in the context of my personal life."

"You have no personal or private life. It is such a long time since you travelled to any place on your own and so long since you saw a river."

"Not seen a river?"

"Maybe you have seen one but only while inaugurating a bridge."

Suddenly she stood up and said, "Let's go."

I thought perhaps it was time for her to go, and that is why she was asking me to leave.

But Mrs. Gandhi again said, "Come, I want to go and see a river with you."

I said, "Normally I shouldn't feel tempted to go out with a lady of your age. But of course you have a different kind of charisma. Not because you are the head of a state. In spite of your age you are still a symbol of youth. There is still a lot of youthfulness in your manners, your gait, and your dress. I have heard that you are very ruthless, but that hasn't left a mark on your face."

"I thought we were discussing the river. Would you like to go and see it?"

"Would all your fifty seven bodyguards accompany us too?"

She smiled slightly and said, "Fifty seven? Did you count them? I didn't know that!"

"Well, once I had seen you at a function at the Rabindra Sadan. There, I had heard that all of fifty seven guards were protecting you. Even when I had gone out to drink water from a public tap, I had seen someone standing there. One could make out that he was a bodyguard. He had told me that nobody came to drink water from that tap because he was standing there. But what could he do? After all he was stationed there."

"Oh such things do happen, do they? Anyway, come on. I will go to the Ganga Ghat all alone today. Its' true that I have been everywhere around the world. I know the world as well as the lines on my palm. But its so long since I stood quietly by the side of a serene river flowing all by itself. Are the *ghat* in Calcutta beautiful?"

"Oh, they are one of the prettiest sights in the world. But you will not be able to go there. Even if you forbid your security guards, they will not listen to you. They'll keep following you from a distance. And besides …"

"Yes?"

"Oh I am slightly hesitant to say the rest. I can say it only if you assure me."

"Yes, go on."

"That killer is standing by the riverside."

"What do you mean?"

"Isn't there a killer waiting for you everywhere? Why else do you have so many security guards?"

Sighing deeply, Mrs. Gandhi replied, "That is of course true. He is there, but this is nothing unnatural. A lot of people have vested interests in getting rid of me. This is true for all heads of nations."

"Yes I know. But the very thought that someone out there is waiting to kill me is very unnerving."

"One doesn't always remember that."

"Having a bodyguard at all times necessarily means accepting that fact consciously or unconsciously."

"Oh one gets used to it. It's a part of the game also."

"There was something unusual about that man standing near the tap in the courtyard of the Rabindra Sadan, something about his posture. That is why I had looked at him with such curiosity. His style was both relaxed and watchful. He looked absent minded and yet vigilant. Surely, he was armed. I could easily have mistaken him for a killer. But he was, in fact, a body guard.

Come to think of it, there is a lot of similarity between a killer and a bodyguard."

Mrs. Gandhi seemed a little disturbed by this remark. She knitted her eyebrows in that very well known style and gazed into empty space for a while. Then she said, "Words just keep building up. I had wanted to go to the river alone."

"Alone!"

"Yes, and you'll show me the way. Probably you know that I am not familiar with the roads in any city. If you leave me here suddenly, I will get lost like a little girl."

"But before that, shouldn't we settle on the matter regarding the killer waiting by the riverside?"

"I have a feeling that there is no killer waiting out there. Didn't you say it was a beautiful place?"

"Remember, it was while Abraham Lincoln was watching a play, that his murderer had sprung on him from the stage itself. Killers have no aesthetic sense –"

"But why should someone want to kill me? Am I not doing my best to save this country?"

"But saving the country is not really the main thing! What matters is who is going to save it! It's the ego of the self that bypasses everything. Until one dies or gets killed, nobody wants to give up playing the role of a saviour."

"We were discussing the river!"

"Not a river, but about standing alone by the river."

"That's right! Why did you think of that suddenly? I have not seen a river for such a long time."

"You had said something related to your personal life, and I had said that you had no private life. That is when the context of the river came up. It is true that you have aeroplanes, you have your commands, you have inauguration dates, but you don't have rivers."

"Does that matter?"

"No."

"Then?"

"Even then, you suddenly wanted to see a river."

"Come on. No one will recognize me. No one will believe it is me. At the most they might say, 'She looks just like Mrs. Gandhi but she cant be Mrs. Gandhi by any means.'"

"Such cases of mistaken identity can happen for film actors but not for you. The papers print your photographs, your face flashed from every angle is published daily!"

"Words only keep building up."

"Come lets' go and test for ourselves."

I was waiting outside the Raj Bhavan. She wrapped a white shawl around herself and came out of the gates. The sun had gone down quite some time back. I had smoked two cigarettes, waiting for her.

Coming closer she said, "I have never walked through these gates. That is why nobody noticed me. They are still guarding my cars."

"I am sure people were streaming in every five minutes, wanting to see you. There must have been lots of demands, lots of requests, lots of protests."

"Yes they were there. But young man, do not consider yourself extra lucky. Remember you are only my guide for the road."

"Well then, the river is right there. You can go straight ahead."

"Are you angry at what I said?"

"Just a while ago, I had told you that at times I did consider myself lucky to accompany ladies for a evening stroll, but that's not relevant in your case."

Hearing this Mrs. Gandhi let out a full throated laughter. It's true that in every adult, man or woman, one can, at times, get a glimpse of a child!

We were walking by the side of the Radio Station, next to the walls of the Stadium. It was a dim, dark evening. There were some people around but no one noticed us. Some young couples passed by, completely engrossed in themselves. A little boy had been following us for quite some time now. Mrs. Gandhi felt a little awkward at not having any money with her. Probably she never carried any money with her, at least not for the past few years.

She looked at me.

I said, "I have some change. But is it proper to give alms?"

"Ask your conscience."

"Oh my conscience gives me different orders at different times. That is why I asked for your opinion."

"I don't teach morality to people."

I gave a ten-paise coin to the beggar boy. As soon as the boy moved away, I said, "Actually I didn't give him the money out of charity. I just wanted him to stop pestering."

"Is he the only beggar in Calcutta?"

"No they are three lakh and one in number!"

"What does "and one" mean?"

"Oh that's including myself."

"What you are a beggar of?"

I kept silent for a while. Then I said, "Actually I was about to say a 'beggar for love'. But then I realised that it would have been a cliché. Again I felt that even if it was a cliché it was indeed true and yet one couldn't really talk of these things."

"Have you never received love?"

"Oh yes I have, but the craving is always there."

"Those who have such cravings can never achieve anything great in their lives."

"Don't you have that weakness?"

"Oh yes I had, once. A long time ago when my mother was ill ... anyway!"

"As a child I had once read a book – "Socrates in an Indian village."

"Oh that doesn't apply in my case."

We came and stopped in one corner of the Eden Gardens. A circular monument stood in the middle of the road – once upon a time it had housed a statue of an English prince but now the pedestal stood empty. Mrs. Gandhi looked at it for a while. A cool breeze was blowing in the air. Suddenly she said, "Oh my guide, where do we go from here?"

I said, "We have to cross the road. Can you manage it?"

Some cars were rushing by, at times there were huge trucks also. It must have been quite some time since she crossed a road by herself, through such a heavy traffic. But she had a smartness in whatever she did. She looked left first and then right, and then slowly crossed the road on to the other side. There was a certain sophistication in her gait. A hurried manner did not suit her.

Instead of going straight towards the Ganges, I strolled past the Fort with her. The wind was blowing even harder now. There was a nip in the air. She wrapped the shawl tightly around her and as if speaking to herself, said, "I can't believe I am in Calcutta and yet have so much time to myself. This city has generally many more complaints than other cities."

I kept quiet. I had run out of matchsticks and couldn't light a cigarette. That was the only thought in my mind at that moment. A man was approaching us from the other side. I noticed the cigarette in his hand, stopped him, and said "Dada, could you please light my cigarette?" The man stopped, caught by surprise. In the little time that I took to light my cigarette he looked at the lady who was perhaps the most famous lady in the country, if not the world. Who knows whether he recognized her or not. He seemed surprised nevertheless, looking first at me and then at her.

She was standing a little off, looking steadfastly at us.

Suddenly a thought flashed in my mind – could this be the killer supposed to be waiting by the riverside? After all, they were all very well informed.

I thanked the man for the light.

No, the man had not recognized her. He went his way again. I looked at Mrs. Gandhi and said, "I smoke a little too often, hope you don't mind."

She brushed aside my remark with a casual gesture of her hand and said, "Why aren't we moving towards the river?"

"Actually, I am not able to decide which place would be most suitable for you." I said. "After all, a tourist guide has so many responsibilities you know."

She said, "Remember, I have come to see a river. And, yes, I look most comfortable on a high dais but that is a different issue."

We crossed a narrow railway track and reached the Strand. The place seemed completely deserted. The river looked dark and serene. A brightly illuminated foreign ship stood close by, and long streaks of light reflected in the nearby waters. The lights from little boats in the distance could be mistaken for glow worms.

Mrs. Gandhi looked at the river and remarked, "Why, nothing much happened really."

"What?"

"I had thought that I would feel something different. But I am only remembering the Farakka, the problems associated with the Calcutta port, the needs of this state, the Second Bridge ..."

I said, "You are still standing on the dais, or possibly at the representative meet in the Raj Bhavan. Mentally, you have not reached the river yet."

She shut her eyes once and then opened them again." I can see the river quite well now."

"Victory or bliss, which one is it?"

"Don't ask me."

"Oh, you are looking so helpless."

"Helpless? Why?" she asked, turning around haughtily.

"Because you cannot make out which one is uppermost in your mind now – victory or bliss."

"I never think of myself. I have to think for the entire country."

"But there is no country here. There is only a river in front of you. Those eternal waters."

She looked ahead at the river, a mixed look of arrogance and secret hurt played on her face. Her lips quivered as if she wanted to say something.

Then rushing down the steps all by herself, she went and stood by the river. Bending a little, she touched the waters.

I thought, she wished to sprinkle a few drops of water on her head. The next minute I realised that she might have gone to the river to confide something very personal to it. After all, she had no one else.

The Wooden Bridge
Sanko

They twisted my hands at the back and tied them with a nylon rope. Then they covered my eyes with a thick black cloth, shoved a ball of cotton into my mouth and sealed my lips with a plaster. I felt two or three men lift me up and carry me some distance before putting me down on a wooden plank.

Then, someone in a very polished voice said, "Now move forward, no need to hurry, just go one step at a time."

I swung one foot down and realized that the plank was only a few feet wide. Beneath that was total emptiness. Was this a bridge? Was there a mountain stream flowing underneath? We had been driving on a dark moonless night, through a mountainous road. The car had stopped suddenly in the middle of a forest. It was quiet all around – in fact there was no sound made by the breeze. As if guessing what was going on in my mind, one of the killers laughed and said, "Yes this is just a temporary bridge over the Teesta river. The waters are running about five to six hundred feet below. One false step and you may be reduced to just a pulp of flesh. Then, lost forever."

I made some muffled sounds while trying to say, "Why are you asking me to cross this bridge?"

The man deciphered the sounds correctly and replied, "Oh, this is just a game of some sort!"

Making the same muffled sounds again, I said, "What if I don't want to play this game?"

"Then you will be pushed hard so that you fall headlong into the river. And we'll light our torches and watch you roll down." A raucous laugh followed.

"But what if I never reach the other end of the plank?"

They laughed again and said, "Oh, you'll see what happens then! Surely something interesting will follow. Come on, now start! We will count just ten. If you don't start moving by then ... One, two, three ..."

I took the first step. It went off quite easily. The wooden plank felt quite sturdy. Placing one foot forward and gripping on to the side of the plank with my toe for gauging the balance, then placing the other foot carefully – this was what was needed to be done each time. One couldn't afford to be absent-minded now. It was not impossible. There were many more difficult games to be played in this life itself.

Even before they could count three, I had moved three steps forward. What did they think of me? Just because they had brought me here by sheer physical force, I would submit to their will? Did they think that I would immediately panic and burst into tears, begging them for mercy? Oh, they don't know me yet.

But, how long was this wooden plank? After all. the *Teesta* river is not all that narrow. I have crossed the Jubilee Bridge a number of times earlier, maybe it is a little narrow near the higher peaks. But, which place is this?

What's happening now? Why are my legs trembling so? My head seems okay, but my legs are trembling violently. As soon as I lift one leg to move forward, the other leg seems unable to support my weight. People can keep standing on one foot for long but it is difficult to move forward in such a posture – not sideways but forward. People don't learn to walk straight right from the day they are born.

"What happened? Why did you stop? Remember, you'll be pushed." Someone shouted from the back

But how could I reply? Didn't they know that my lips were sealed? Besides, there was no answer to this question.

"You'll either be pushed or shot down." They repeated. "You cannot remain still. We'll start counting ten again ... One, two, three ..."

Oh, if only they would give me a stick to keep my balance. Huh – a stick! They had not even kept my hands free! As a child, whenever I used to walk over a wall or on the railway tracks, my hands would, by themselves, spread out on both sides, like a pair of wings!

Even if my eyes were uncovered now, it would not be an easy task to cross such a narrow bridge in such deep darkness! Why did they still blindfold me? Its said that if need be, people can even see in the dark. Had my eyes been uncovered, I would at least be able to see the darkness. Wasn't that something to be seen? There are so many different types of darkness. But there isn't a place in this world where one could see pure, unadulterated darkness!

My legs are trembling violently now. I don't think I'll be able to make it! Just a while back, I was almost losing my step, and falling off. This is really an unfair game!

Anyway, I don't think they can hit me with their stick any more. I am sure I have come far away from their reach now. Of course, they could still shoot me down! But I am not going to die from their bullets! If they start counting again, I will jump off this plank as soon as they reach nine.

"Neelu, Neelu!"

Wasn't that was my father's voice? But my father had died quite some time back. He couldn't possibly call me from across this river, even if one believed in the existence of the human soul. Was it a bird of some kind that it would fly across this dark river? This was just a fantasy, such things generally occur in stories and novels. Have I then unconsciously become a child again and started seeking my father's help?

"Neelu, Neelu, aren't you able to move? Shall I hold your hand?"

"Baba, my hands are tied! Do you also have hands?"

"No, I don't. But you can't afford to stop now. Come, move forward slowly. Imagine that your mother is sitting here – just a little further away."

"Where does Ma stay? Does she stay in the front or at the back?"

A gust of wind suddenly blew. Till now one couldn't even feel any breeze. It was quite warm indeed, but it wouldn't be particularly nice for a strong wind to blow now. As soon as I lift a leg, the rest of my body feels almost as light as a dried petal. Even a gust of wind could now blow me off. I am not being able to move forward. No, I really can't!

From somewhere behind me, I could hear those men counting away "One, two, three ... seven, eight ..."

"Neelu, Neelu, don't jump!"

Was that my mother's voice? No, it seemed different, but very familiar. Who are you?

"Neelu, don't jump! Come, come forward. Can't you recognize me Neelu?"

"Oh, Rini, I really couldn't recognize you at first. And yet I had thought that I would never forget you all my life! How strange indeed!"

"Neelu, did you really forget me?"

"No Rini, I didn't. But then I didn't remember you for a long time also. Where did you get lost all these days?

"It wasn't me who got lost, it was you who went away so far."

"Rini, my eyes are covered. I can't see you. Are you still like what you were earlier? With that look of wonder in your eyes, and your body as frail as a whirling feather?"

"Don't talk Neelu. Come forward and hold my hand."

"I can't Rini. I can't do it any more. See, how long it is taking me to lift my foot."

"There was a time when you had left everything behind and come running to me!"

"Did I come running? Or was it you who had attracted me like a magnet? Can't you pull me like that once more?"

"So many years have passed in between ... Neelu, don't walk forward, move sideways. You don't need to lift your foot. You can just drag one foot and move on. Your legs wouldn't be trembling then. I have kept my hand stretched out for you."

"True, it is really easier walking with my body turned to one side. Rini, how did you know it? Did you ever have to cross a bridge like this?"

There was no reply. Rini hadn't come. Was that my subconscious again? This whole idea of walking with my body turned to a side – was it Rini's suggestion or did I think of it myself? I hadn't thought of Rini for many years now. Rini was lost – or had I myself moved away far? There was a time when I had been so desperate to reach out as close as possible to her. How close really? The rays of the sun travel millions of miles before throwing themselves headlong on the human body, and then seeping through every hair-root on the skin, they light up the dark world of the marrow and the blood-veins lying underneath, had it been like that?

No, I hadn't lit the spark. Rini had. It was on a quiet afternoon, while sitting in their living room on the first floor, she had raised a hand in front of my eyes and asked "Do you know what is on my fingertip?"

I had felt time freeze into eternity there.

Yet then, how did we lose each other? No, I will not leave Rini again. I must have her this time. I will imagine that Rini is standing only ten steps away from me, with her finger raised, I have to reach her.

"Neelu, remember, I am exactly ten steps away from you. Just count your steps and move forward."

"Rini, when I reach you, will you remove the cover from my eyes at least? I wish to see you once, please."

"In a way, its good that your eyes are covered. Otherwise you would have felt dizzy trying to look down. There's a faint streak of light shining in the waters running deep below."

"I will not look down. I will only keep looking at the tip of your finger."

My legs didn't tremble as I moved those ten steps forward. But, Rini was not there. Where was that noise coming from? Was it from the waters deep below?

Oh my subconscious, couldn't you have been a little more powerful and created Rini in true flesh and blood? What a fool I was! Why did I say that Rini was only ten steps away? Had I imagined instead that Rini was standing fifty steps away, or even further – perhaps on the other side of the pool, with her nimble finger raised towards the Orion in the sky, I might have been drawn to reach the other side . But like a miser, I have uttered a number as small as ten and lost my Rini completely. Even if I rummage through my sub conscious now, Rini will never come back, never!

"Hey, you idiot, why did you get stuck?" A harsh voice floated from the back "Have we come to spend the entire night here? Shall we open fire?"

Are they watching me with their torch light? They are six in all, I had counted them. There was no way of resisting them. Are they waiting for me to fall off the plank? Or have they placed a bet among themselves?

Often, there's a scene in the movies where the hero suddenly misses a step and then spectators are left holding their breath in anxious excitement. But the hero doesn't fall finally. He manages to clutch on to a part of the bridge and keeps hanging from it while wild crocodiles with their wide – open jaws keep waiting in the waters below. And even in that kind of a precarious situation, the hero manages to finally scramble up.

But if I fall now, I'll not be able to climb back. My hands are tied. I can't even hold onto the plank with my teeth. I can't afford to make even the slightest mistake. In any case, I'm not a hero and this is not a film. This is a desperate effort to live.

Of course, it is not absolutely necessary that I live. A little red grasshopper sitting on a fresh, green pumpkin swinging from the thatched roof of a hut, with it's wings fluttering in the breeze. How reassured and happy it looks as it sits quietly, even though a sparrow could snatch it away any moment. Why is this scene haunting me constantly?

How much further do I have to go? Have I come half way? Its only a matter of a moment really. If I jump down now, then I'll not need to endure the pain. A person falling from a great height is known to die from suffocation because of the air pressure at that altitude. Actually getting lost in the seas is a far better way of dying.

Oh, its swaying now, I can feel the plank swaying under my feet. Are they purposely swinging it from that end? Then this must be their game. They will not let me cross over to the other side at any cost. They will upset my balance midway. Or maybe this long wooden plank with possibly no support underneath could be bending somewhere in between. Yes, it's sloping here and its swaying now. So, it will not be those men, it will be this fragile plank of wood that will eventually throw me into the river.

"Neelu, Neelu, you must keep moving your body also, otherwise you will not be able to keep your balance."

"Who is that – Gaganda! where did you come from?"

"Oh, I don't have time to talk, Neelu. Just keep moving your body, and move forward, a few steps at a time."

"Oh, I just can't do that any more Gaganda. The waters are pulling me down, I am about to fall ..."

"No, no, you can, you have to do it Neelu. Keep swaying with the plank and stretch out a leg. Don't lose heart, pull yourself up. You will be able to do it Neelu, you surely will."

Oh my sub-conscious, what is all this? Where did you get Gaganda from? How can I sway, stretch out my leg, and also gather strength in my heart and body? How can I do all this at the same time? Do I know some kind of magic? Gaganda had taught me so many wrong things in my college days. He had said, 'Learn to speak to villagers in their own dialect'. He had said 'Arm yourself for the revolution'. He had asked us to forsake love in our own personal lives. He had said that 'For the sake of an ideal – be ready to kill even your friend.' All that was to be done at the same time – it had set my head reeling. I had felt puzzled, I had turned blind. And when I opened my eyes again,

I saw that Gaganda himself hadn't followed any of those. He had settled down to an easy and comfortable life. On seeing me open my eyes he had even said, "Who are you? I don't know you!"

Why are these images of Baba. Rini and Gaganda coming up in my mind now? Is it symbolising some thing? Crossing a dangerous bridge over such a fast – flowing river in the dark itself seems to be symbolic. 'Living a life is like walking over a sharp-edged razor' – some such ponderous words have found a place in the Upanishads. Oh bull – shit! Had this not been symbolic, I could have lived easily. Six ugly, terrible murderers have brought me here by force; I don't know why they are so angry with me. Instead of shooting me down with a single bullet, they are playing this terrible, dirty, game. I know that at the slightest misstep, death awaits me. This is the hard and only truth! I think this night in my life will probably never end!

"One, two, three, four ..."

– Wait, please, I am coming. Is there anybody who doesn't wish to live? Everybody strives so desperately to remain alive. I'm coming, wait ...

The plank beneath my feet has suddenly stopped swaying. I must have come half the way. It's very warm now. It would be nice if I could take my shirt off. It is so dark that it wouldn't really matter if I took off my trousers as well. At least my body would have felt much lighter. They have done at least one good thing, unknowingly. They have let me come bare foot. My toes are now clutching on to the wooden plank in much the same way as our primitive ancestors did.

"Neelu, don't be afraid. I am always with you."

"Baba, you have come again? Baba, didn't I get once lost in unknown streets even when you were with me? And wasn't it I myself who finally found the way out?

"Neelu, even at such times, a parental love surrounds the child. But children don't seem to understand that, because affection always moves downward, so they forget their own parents and turn their attention to their own children ..."

Oh my dear subconscious! Why did you bring back Baba? This will only make me more weak. I could not be present when he died. I hadn't obeyed much of his good advices .I had remained preoccupied with my friends and lost myself in a strange restless world. But, was this the right time to feel sorry for all that? If you have to bring someone, then bring Rini. If nothing else, at least her voice will restore my will to live.

How strange indeed, it's my own sub conscious and yet I am not being able to control it. I asked for Rini, and it brought me Gaganda. My dear conscience, are you also, like these six terrible men, trying to play a trick on me? Why else did you bring Gaganda now? Men like Gaganda would always preach such high-sounding platitudes! Those words might be able to take a few to the doors of liberation, but then what about the hundreds or thousands who would fall into that endless pit? Who would keep track of them? I belong to that large group! And, yet I want to live. I promise, I swear by Ma Kali, that I want to live. I am even ready to live like one of those who live by the roadside and eat off others' plates. But I don't want to fall into a river and let my body be shattered into pieces!

Right foot, left foot, right, left, right, left ... my sub conscious has ceased to exist. My entire concentration is now focused on my feet. My eyes are tied, my hands and mouth are also tied. Only my feet are uncovered. I will have to live only with these feet. I will not be able to retreat now. I will not be able to stop either. Do they still have their guns pointed at me, are they still watching me with the help of their torch light? How much more, oh how much more do I have to walk, who knows! It's so long that I have been walking!

I can hear some voices from nearby. Real human voices, and not that of my subconscious. It's pure and simple reality. Have I then reached the other end of the plank? Am I still alive? Some men seem to be standing on this side of the river too, I can hear them talking. Thank God, they have not blocked my ears, I can hear quite clearly.

"Buck up, buck up." Someone said. "He has come, he has come – just a few steps more!"

Another said, "My God, the rascal finally made it!"

Yet another said, "One is to four! Didn't I say that the will to live in every man is very strong. This man will definitely cross over. Don't forget, you have to pay me my share of the bet."

I stopped. The voices were familiar. They were the same men who a while back, had been behind me; they are the ones who had brought me here by force. There must have been some safer, more convenient, and shorter bridge nearby. They must have crossed over that and reached this side of the shore. Its only people like them who get to know of such bridges, even in the dead of the night. Yes, these people get everything easily in life.

"Why did you stop?" One of them asked. "Come on, walk boldly now. There's nothing to be scared of any more."

Another said, "We had never thought that this man could really complete this job. He ought to be given some kind of a reward."

Yet another said, "Certainly, we know how to show the sportsman spirit, don't we? As soon as he puts his foot on this side of the shore, we'll declare him a winner. Hey, what would you like to have as a reward? A house built on two acres of land, a foreign trip, an agency with a medical firm, or a contract for building a road – tell us what you would like."

My legs felt weak, they were trembling violently. I suddenly remembered what I had once heard in my childhood – about that measured three feet length on the trunk of a date tree. Its difficult for a layman to climb the tree, and the last three feet seem to be the toughest. Like a boat on the verge of capsizing near the shores, I too seemed unable to move forward. No, I just couldn't move a step anymore.

"What are you doing dear?" My sub-conscious said. "There is no water under the bridge here. It's just hard, dry mud. You can easily run over the plank now and reach the other end."

I laughed and turned around.

These people had promised to reward me once I reached that end. This is their game.

Everybody wants to live, I too want to. But shouldn't there be some kind of a pride in one's own life? Otherwise, living like just parasites ... only a worldly life, always scrambling towards a carrot being dangled in front? I have to play the game their way!

As soon as I turned around and took the first step, I heard a loud uproar behind me.

"What is this?" The men called out excitedly. "Has this fellow gone mad? You idiot, which way are you going? Come on this side, quick, you're saved, and alive ..."

My lips were sealed, yet I said – "Just watch me. I'll start playing my own game now."

Virtue and Sin
Dharmadhormo

It had started raining since the morning, a drizzle that had stopped in between, but the sky had not still cleared up. After continuing this way throughout the day, it started raining cats and dogs towards the evening.

On such days, one did not feel like going out. It was an ideal occasion for relaxing at home. However, on such days, incidents of thefts and dacoity were found to be rampant. There was no end to people streaming in and out of local police stations.

This locality had no electricity as yet. Two hurricane lamps burnt dimly on the table nearby. At times, a strong gust of wind from outside almost extinguished the light.

Rahman Sahib looked around once, and ordered, "Shut all doors and windows."

Then, keeping his diary aside, he put his feet up on the table. Loosening the belt around his waist, he muttered, "Enough! I have done enough work for the day." Then he raised his voice a little, and called out again "Ali, Ali go get me some *muri* –. "

Ali was a thin, squeaky man. One could not tell his age from his face. He could be thirty or even fifty years old. At the slightest hint of a command he would start scampering around hastily.

Ali came and stood by the inspector's table. Rehman Sahib was a large man, very fair, with a well trimmed moustache. He spoke in a thunderous voice, but at heart he was nice. Even the common man could speak his mind out in Rehman's presence.

Flashing out a rupee note from his pocket, Rehman Sahib said, "Go get me some *muri* for eight annas and fried cutlets with the rest. Make sure the cutlets are piping hot. If they are not, then get them fried fresh, alright?"

Folding his hands together in respect, Ali said, "Yes Sir."

"But remember, if you take more than ten minutes, I'll chop off your head" Rehman Sahib said with a smile on his face. "Now, run, and don't forget to take the umbrella."

As soon as Ali left, Rehman Sahib started moving his knees to and fro, absent mindedly. Sub-inspector Dhiren Saha had been down with fever for the last three days. Ever since the only literate constable Jagdish Saha had been transferred from this *thana*, no one had come in his place. For the last few days, Rehman Sahib had been handling everything himself.

On the other side of the table, some people sat quietly on a bench. They were all thugs, thieves and smugglers, about five of them – arrested during the day. All of them knew that the inspector was now hungry. It would not be wise to disturb him at such a moment.

Constables Haranath and Siddiqui were standing outside the

door exchanging news and munching *khaini*. Haranath was on night duty today. Siddiqui was going to leave any moment now. But having heard the Inspector Sahib send for cutlets and *muri*, he decided to stay back for a while.

Ali returned quite quickly. Spreading a newspaper on Rehman's table, he poured the *muri* over it. The cutlets potato were sizzling.

Popping a handful into his mouth, Rehman Sahib said, "What about green chillies? Didn't you get some chillies?"

"No Sir." Ali said.

"When will you ever learn? Tell me, can anyone have *muri* without green chillies? Run. Get me some chillies – quick."

Ali almost ran out of the room.

Raising his voice again Rehman Sahib said, "Come on Haranath, Siddiqui, where are the two of you? Come, have some *muri*."

The group of thugs, thieves and smugglers sat quietly on the bench facing him. Rehman glanced in their direction. After all, he was a gentleman. He couldn't possibly eat alone in public without offering some to others.

"Haranath, give those people a handful each. They have been waiting for long." He called out.

This idea of offering the motley group *muri* bought with Rehaman Sahib's own money was something that Haranath disliked immensely. Taking just a handful he looked despondently at the convicts and said,

"Here, take this. The Inspector Sahib has given this to you."

By the time Ali returned again – the *muri* was almost finished.

Rehman laughed and said, "*Arre*, what shall we do now? Will you get me some more *muri*? After all there's nothing like crisp *muri* on a rainy day."

Another man had come with Ali this time. He was standing alone in the dark.

"Who is that?" Rahman Sahib asked.

"Huzoor, its me – Pratap Singh ..." the man answered, stepping forward.

Rehman looked at the man standing before him. A lean frame clad in a dhoti – it seemed he had not eaten for a long time. He knew no language other than Bangla. It was a little difficult to believe that his name was Pratap Singh. But over the years a lot of people from different parts of the country had settled down in Murshidabad. During the era of the Nawabs, so many Rajputs, Pathans, and Punjabis had come here in search of work, many of their descendents had by now changed and joined the feeble clan of Bengalis and become part of the local crowd.

Pratap Singh had earlier been a petty thief. Now he was a police informer. He had recently opened a shop in Jiyaganj selling *bidis*.

Rehman Sahib didn't like Singh's presence at this moment. This man often brought stray information from various sources.

"What do you want?" he asked.

Pratap Singh took a step forward and said "Sir, I have confirmed news."

"What is it? Tell me."

Coming closer, Pratap Singh began to whisper something in Rehman Sahib's ears. Rehman Sahib listened attentively as he kept nibbling at the bits of *muri* spread on his table. At one point, he looked excited and said, "Really?"

"Sir, I have seen with my own eyes."

"But you had seen him many times earlier too, isn't it?"

"There is no mistaking this time Huzoor."

Rehman Sahib stood up and started tightening his belt. There was a certain urgency and excitement in his movement as he called out –"Darwaza!"

Ali came running "Ji Huzoor!"

"Come with me! Who else will come? Haranath!"

"Huzoor, who will stay back at the *thana* then!" Haranath said.

Correct! Someone had to stay back at the *thana*. That was Haranath's duty. On the other hand, they needed an armed constable to accompany them. Ali was of no use. Then they might as well take Siddiqui with them.

Siddiqi's duty was over for the day. Still, he did not refuse to accompany Rehman Sahib.

The next moment, three cycles wheeled out on the road. In spite of having made several requests to the Zilla S. P., this *thana* was yet to receive a jeep. Even the inspector had to move around on a cycle! Today, Siddiqui offered to carry Pratap Singh on the pillion of his cycle.

Pratap Singh had brought news of Shivmangal. Even after many desperate attempts, the police had failed to arrest him all these years. Had Shivmangal been just an ordinary criminal, Rehman Sahib would not have set out on such a stormy night. An arrest warrant in his name had come from a place no less than Delhi. Shivmangal was wanted on grounds of stealing and transporting valuables to countries abroad. He had even stolen treasures from the museum in Hazar Duari!

It was not raining hard, but a strong wind still blew from time to time. The road ahead lay in pitch darkness. Rehman Sahib turned around and asked, "Which way do we go now?"

Pratap said, "Huzoor, its just behind Hatkhola, near the bank of the Ganga. He's right there – in Chapala's room."

Rehman was surprised. He knew Chapala. She was one of the three or four prostitutes who lived in the colony behind Hatkhola. Only the very poor visited such places. What was Shivmangal doing there?

Even though Shivmangal was a dreaded thief, he was quite old now, certainly not less than sixty. He had been evading the police for many years. Why would he be visiting prostitutes still?

Pratap said, "Huzoor, Chapala is his daughter!"

Rehman was amazed. Whatever the man was today – a thief or a scoundrel, he had heard that Shivmangal actually hailed from an aristocratic family. One of his uncles was a prospering businessman in Calcutta. Another had even gone abroad during the days of the freedom movement. Had he been alive till after Independence, he would certainly have become a minister. Could a person from such a family be a common thief?

Shivmangal's surname was Singh, but now some members of his family had started writing Sinha instead, and assumed a Bengali identity.

Rehman looked around. Most of the rooms in the locality

were in darkness. Probably, the women inside had not got any clients on such a stormy night. They must have shut their doors and fallen asleep with the cool breeze wafting into their room. The doors and windows in Chapala's room were also shut, but a streak of light could be seen coming from under the door.

Getting off from the cycle, Rehman Sahib started walking towards the door.

Turning to Pratap, he said, "How did you get the news?"

Without feeling the least bit embarrassed Pratap said, "Huzoor I have been visiting Chapala from time to time."

"Did you come here today also?"

"Yes Huzoor."

"And then?"

"I saw someone in Chapala's room. I got curious and peeped over the fence at the back. I saw ..."

He broke off in the middle of his speech and said, "Sir, please go ahead and knock. I will not go any further."

Saying this he turned around swiftly and vanished in the dark.

Rehman watched him for a while and laughed silently to himself. Could someone ever get another man like this Pratap Singh? Once a thief himself, now he helped the police in tracking down others like him. He visited Chapala frequently but not other girls like her. If he had been a regular here, he could easily have gone into another room. He must have had a soft corner for Chapala. Yet, he had gone to inform the police about her father, possibly in the hope of a reward.

After all this would be over, he would possibly visit Chapala some day and express sympathy for her father's arrest.

"Go and guard the back of the house." Rehman Sahib ordered Ali and Siddiqui. "In case the old man tries to escape, just shoot him down."

Saying this, he went and knocked on Chapala's door. Hushed voices audible from the room till now, suddenly stopped. When he knocked once again, Rehman heard Chapala say "No, it will not be possible today. I have an all – night customer with me right now."

Rehman Sahib knocked on the door with a greater force this time. As soon as the door opened a bit, he pushed himself in.

Shivmangal was sitting in the centre of the room. He had just started eating. On seeing the Inspector, he stood up immediately. A meal of rice, dal and boiled potatos was laid out on a bone china plate on the floor in front of him. Shivmangal had just taken a mouthful or two. By his side were two large silver bowls containing *paneer* and curd. He stood with his hands still unwashed. Chapala's face looked pale frightened.

"Siddiqi, Siddiqi" Rehman called out.

Siddiqui entered the room with a pointed rifle. "Go and stand next to him." Rehman Sahib ordered

Siddiqui walked over to where Shivmangal stood and clutched him by his shoulders.

Chapala, almost in tears now, pleaded, "*Babu*, please let him finish his meal ..."

Rehman Sahib said, "But, a *musselman* has touched him now. Can he still eat that food?"

"Huzoor I am very hungry today." Shivmangal cried. "I will not be able to walk if I don't eat properly."

"Siddiqui, let him go." Rehman Sahib ordered again.

Shivmangal sat down immediately. Taking two or three mouthfuls of food he said, "Chapala, ask the Inspector Sahib to sit down. Offer him a chair."

There was no place to sit in Chapala's room – other than her bed. Rehman Sahib would not sit on it. Chapala laid out another soft rug on the floor. It was rather funny for Rehman Sahib to sit facing an offender on the same floor; but he accepted the offer and sat down.

"Huzoor, would you like to have some water, or maybe a cup of tea?" Chapala asked.

"No."

Shivmangal was now concentrating on his food. Chapala went inside and brought him some rice in a bowl. "Have some more rice." She said.

"Alright. Do you have some more *Dal*?"

"Yes."

Rehman kept staring at the scene in front of him. Here was a daughter serving food to her father with such caring hands. Chapala now looked like any other girl from a middle class family. She didn't have any rouge on her cheeks, nor was she wearing a cheap nylon saree. She was dressed in a simple white saree with a red border – the sort one wears everyday. All this – even though she had referred to her father as a all – night client!

Rehman Sahib looked at Shivmanangal and smiled to himself. How many residents of this locality could afford even a set of cheap crockery leave alone such good quality porcelain! There were two silver bowls also. Not surprising, after all they were from an aristocratic family! Of course, Chapala had served water in an ordinary glass. Shivmangal must have made a great fortune. Who knows how he spent it? Why else would his daughter have to hire a room in this locality – Hatkhola!

Shivmangal finished his meal. Scraping out the last crumb of food from his plate he said, "Huzoor, may I please go and wash my hands now?"

Rehman Sahib gestured to Siddiqui with his eyes, asking him to accompany the man. Then he turned to Ali and said, "Go and wash that plate and bowl yourself. We have to take them to the *thana*."

At the very thought of having to wash a Hindu's plate, Ali scowled. Seeing him hesitate Rehman Sahib lashed out, "Do as I say."

Chapala intervened, "Huzoor, I'll wash them myself. The tap is just outside the door."

"Where are the rest of his belongings?" Rehman asked her.

"I have no idea Huzoor."

Rehman looked at Chapala with eyes full of anger. He was certain that all kinds of people including thieves and dacoits visited her room regularly. She wouldn't have survived if she had felt intimidated by such people. It was as if she had accepted everything as part of her life!

"Is Shivmangal your father?" he asked.

"Yes."

"Where's your mother?"

"She has been gone for long now."

"Does Shivmangal live here? Doesn't he have a place of his own somewhere else?"

"He had, once upon a time. Now he doesn't."

As soon as Shivmangal returned, Rehman Sahib stood up. Without another word he swung around and slapped him hard.

This sudden spurt of anger that he felt towards Shivmangal was not because the man was a thief. He had seen many such scoundrels in his profession. But he just couldn't bear the sight of this man sitting and enjoying a meal at his daughter's place even after driving her to prostitution. On top of that he didn't seem to have any resentment or sympathy for her!

Having received such a sudden blow, Shivmangal lost his balance and sat down on the floor, resting his head in his hands. Even though most of his hair had turned white, his body was still quite strong. No one could make out that he was a thief just by looking at him. Had he dressed well and mingled with other gentlemen, he would have easily commanded respect from one and all. That was in fact the strategy he used for stealing valuables from people's houses. Using some pretext or disguise he would make his way into old aristocratic homes and start removing priceless treasures one by one.

"Where are the stolen goods?" Rehman thundered.

"Please don't hit me Huzoor. I'll take them out for you."

Crouching low, Shivamangal pulled out a bag from under the bed. As soon as the bag was opened, a number of things rolled out, bright and shining silver knives and forks, an ivory snuff-box, two jade dolls, and a fashionable knife with a beautifully designed cover.

"Is this all?" Rehman asked.

"Yes, Huzoor."

Well, if this was indeed the entire booty, he could be jailed for a maximum period of six months only, but Shivmangal was a fish of much deeper waters. Apprehending an arrest any moment, he was always prepared with only a few stolen articles at hand.

Seeing Rehman Sahib lift his hand again, Shivmangal bent low and said, "Believe me Huzoor, I have nothing else. Only a few more wooden dolls, but they are not very expensive."

The dolls were taken out of the wooden cupboard. Shivmangal took them out himself. They were all terracotta figurettes probably removed from some ancient temple, the kind that was of immense value to foreigners.

Rehman Sahib could make out that this was only the second list of stolen goods. This too was an act. The most valuable things had not been brought out yet. Shivmangal's eyes moved restlessly.

Rehman Sahib ordered Siddiqui and Ali to search the room thoroughly. Chapala didn't have many belongings; a tin suitcase, a clothes rack, and a wooden almirah were all that she had. It didn't take long to search those. In the end, nothing except a silver spoon was found. Chapala had probably hidden this without her father's knowledge, one could easily make that out from the look in Shivmangal's eyes.

Rehman lit a torch and started searching the corners. It wouldn't be surprising if he found a hole somewhere on the floor. He looked at every nook and corner to see if he could find one.

In an alcove a little above the door, he noticed a stone idol covered with some flowers and *bel* leaves. Each time the light fell in that direction, something glittered. Possibly something was hidden there.

Flashing the torch in that direction and holding the beam of light still, Rehman thought for a while. Then he told Chapala "There's an idol there. Move it. I want to see what is behind it."

"How can I touch the deity, Sir?" Chapala asked.

Indeed, how could a prostitute dare to touch a deity? There were too many restrictions in their religion.

"Then, who kept that idol there?"

"I had requested the Brahmin priest to keep it."

Rehman Sahib began to repent now. He wished he had brought Haranath instead of Siddiqui. Haranath was a Brahmin, even though he was a policeman. It wouldn't have mattered if he had touched the idol. As for himself, Siddiqui, or Ali, touching a Hindu deity was sacriligious.

Shivmangal said, "Huzoor, I'll clear that place so that you can see for yourself and feel assured. Why should you let any doubt creep into your mind?"

Yes, Shivmangal could touch a deity inspite of being a thief. Possibly, that would not be a blasphemy. But his daughter could not! Holding the idol tightly in his hand, he quickly moved aside the flowers and leaves. There was nothing at the back.

"I told you Huzoor. See there is nothing else."

Rehman Sahib looked absent-mindedly at Shivmangal's hands. Suddenly he felt a shock of surprise. Turning the torch light carefully in that direction he let out a cry of alarm.

It was a small idol of the goddess Kali, an exquisitely beautiful idol with its eyes and tongue made of pure gold. But it was not only because of this, it had a greater value for some other reason. Two weeks ago an idol of Kali had gone missing from the prayer room of the Zamindar of Akandapur, and the news had been flashed in bold letters in all the important newspapers. A circular had been sent out to all the *thanas* and a prize of two and a half thousand rupees would be awarded to the person who recovered it.

Even before anybody could say anything, Shivmangal said – "Huzoor, I had bought this for my daughter from a fair at Natore. It is designed in bronze."

Rehman frowned angrily He had never imagined that he would have found such a prized thing here.

"You son of a –, give it to me. Give it to me right now." He roared.

Shivmangal held on to the idol tightly – "Huzoor, don't touch a Hindu God."

"What? A God? Or, a stolen booty?"

"Huzoor, we worship this daily."

Rehman Sahib withdrew his outstretched hand. This was a very puzzling affair indeed. Who could tell, whether by touching the Kali idol he would be sparking off a communal problem? It was true that the idol had been worshipped with flowers and Bel leaves. But Shivmangal was also an extremely shrewd man.

Rehman's hands were now getting impatient to beat the hell out of this man. But he could not hit him. Shivmangal was still holding the deity in his hand. Who knew whether it was a sin to touch him now?

"Sir, don't touch that." Ali cautioned Rehman Sahib

"Examine it carefully." Rehman ordered Siddiqui. "See, if it matches with the description of the Goddess Kali that was stolen from the Zamindar's house in Akandapur."

"Sir it matches perfectly. There's no doubt about that." Siddiqui said.

In the meantime, having heard about the arrival of the police, some locals had begun to collect around the house. Stepping outside the room, Rehman addressed them.

"Is there any Brahmin among you?" He asked

Without a word, all of them ran away. Even Rehman Sahib knew that this was a predominantly Muslim area, and that there were not too many Brahmins here.

Maybe that man who fried cutlets by the road side was a Brahmin. But where could he be found at this time of the night?"

Turning around, Rehman Sahib asked Chapala – "Has this idol been worshipped daily?"

"Sir, it's a living god. If we don't worship it daily, will we not die horrible deaths?"

How strange indeed was all this! It didn't hurt their conscience to steal a living god, and yet it had to be worshipped everyday. Had Shivmangal brought the idol for the purpose of mere worship, or had he wanted to sell it?"

"Who performs the Puja?" he asked.

"The Brahmin priest, Huzoor. He lives on the other side of the river."

So, there was a Brahmin priest somewhere across the river

who even visited a prostitutes' quarter to perform a puja! A great man indeed! Where could one contact him now?"

Rehman looked at Shivmangal and said, "Let it remain in your hand. Come on, let us go outside."

"Huzoor, will you take it away by force?" Shivmangal asked raising his voice.

Had this happened during the day, this man would probably have tried to spark off a communal riot. But, now there were very few people around.

Rehman Sahib said, "You know, I have orders to shoot you down, if needed. Come on."

Siddiqui was about to hit Shivmangal but Rehman stopped him. He didn't want to engage in any kind of physical contact. But it wouldn't be forbidden to touch him with a rifle, after all, it was made of just wood and iron. "Push him from the back with the rifle butt." He ordered.

"Inspector Sir, if you remove this idol from my room, what will happen to me?" Chapala asked, with tears in her eyes.

"Listen, this belonges to someone else. Now move, get off my way." Rehman replied.

Shivmangal refused to go on a cycle. How could he ride a cycle with a Muslim while holding a Hindu deity in his hand?"

Rehman Sahib ordered, "Walk – all of you."

The rain had by now changed to a heavy down pour. Dark clouds had gathered in the sky. They were to walk about seven miles in this weather. What else could be done! Had Haranath been here, Rehman Sahib would not have faced such a problem.

Then again, how was he going to keep that Hindu deity, a living god, in the *thana*! Who knew what was forbidden in the Hindu religion – and what actually amounted to committing a sin!

On reaching the *thana*, Rehman Sahib decided that he would immediately wake up the Sub inspector, Dhiren Saha, explain the situation to him, and then hand over charge to his Sub Inspector and Haranath. God knows, he had never been in such a difficult situation before!

The roads were by now mushy with rain water. Nothing could be seen clearly. Only the deafening howls of wolves in the distance pierced the silence of the night.

Suddenly, Shivmangal stopped and said "Inspector Sahib, take the silver with you. Just let me go."

"Come on you scoundrel." Rehman roared back.

"What will you all do with this statue?" Shivmangal asked again.

"Move on, move on."

"I promise you I will not sell it. Huzoor, it's a living god. May I be struck with leprosy if I sell it. Let me go, please."

"I said – move." Rehman ordered again.

Shivmangal suddenly lifted his hand in the air and muttered "Then let it go to hell". He flung the idol onto the ground and heard it fall with a thud. Obviously, he did not want to keep any evidence with him.

All this while, the three men could not touch him. But there was nothing to stop them now. Their pent-up anger burst out.

"Beat him hard. Beat up the rascal" said Siddiqui, hitting Shivmanagal on his back with the butt of his rifle. Ali too kept punching him, laying his hands wherever he could. Whether it was for real or whether he feigned it nobody knew, but Shimangal immediately lost consciousness.

Holding the torch in his hands, Rehman ran to where the statue lay on the ground. After some search, he discovered it. The idol lay on the mud on, its jewelled eyes glittering in the torchlight.

Rehman Sahib bent down to pick it up, but controlled himself at the last moment. There was no one here – but even then, why touch it?"

After all, it was a different religion, a different god – what if all this lost its sanctity at his touch?

Rehman turned around and ordered his men. "Here, put that man on your cycle and take him to the *thana* with you. Tie up his arms and legs first. But be very careful, Shivmangal is a very crafty man. Put him in the lock-up. Then go and see if you can find that Brahmin *meshir* who fries cutlets in that roadside shop. If you can't get him, just bring Haranath along. Inform the Sub Inspector Sahib."

After they left, Rehman Sahib kept standing alone in pitch darkness, surrounded by swarms of stinging mosquitoes. His cycle lay by the roadside. Had that stolen item been anything else, he would have easily picked it up and carried it to the *thana* on his own cycle. After all, it was only a statue.

"A statue? Hordes of men and women prostrated and wept before this idol – some even made vows to be fulfilled in case

God granted their wish. Some said it was a living god."

But, right now that god was lying in the mud. Would it be a sin to wash it and keep it in a cleaner place? Shivmangal had flung it onto the ground – hadn't his heart trembled even once? And to think that it would have got sold off to the foreigner just as a piece of antique?

Rehman Sahib flicked the torch once again, pointing the light on the Idol's eyes. The eyes and tongue of the stone idol were made of gold and harmonised so beautifully with the rest of the body!

Was it a new new moon tonight? Suddenly, Rehman Sahib started feeling somewhat scared. Ashamed at his own weakness, he tried to brush off his nervousness. Right from his childhood he had studied the ways and rituals of the Hindus. His own religion was far from all this. Even then he felt a slight tremor under his skin. He could not leave this place – he would have to wait even in this darkness and suffer the stinging mosquito bites until Haranath arrived.

Suddenly, a thought flashed in Rehman's mind. He realised that within the separate circles that existed in the life of every individual – Shivmangal, Chapala, Siddiqui, Ali, Haranath or even his own – there was enough place for virtue and vice to coexist side by side. It was as if at that moment he had stepped outside the circle of his own life. As if he was standing completely alone in this large universe. The fact that he could stand on this new moon night guarding the deity belonging to a different religion, made him feel somewhat proud.

Nobody was watching him now, but that really didn't matter!

Our Manorama
Amader Manorama

In this town of ours' known as Khepu, Jaguda's tea shop is very well known. Of course there are two other tea shops here, but those are actually restaurants. Both of them are inside the market – one next to the shoe shop and the other next to the Bansari Cinema hall. Along with tea, those restaurants also serve cutlets, but the air inside stinks of onions and stale fish. It is really nauseating, even flies from the open roadside gutters swarm the tables. It's a wonder that people want to spend their money to eat at such places!

Of course our own Jaguda's shop is totally different. It has no proper shape or form. Located far away from the market, it is actually a small tin shed which has only four unstable wooden tables and eight chairs inside. Two more wooden benches are placed diagonally near the door to accommodate larger groups, even though that happens only on rare occasions.

Most of the time one could get only tea and salted biscuits in

Jaguda's shop, but between six and eight O clock, he could even get a plate of mutton ghugnee for just 30 paise, a dish so delicious that one could feel its taste lingering several hours after eating it. We can bet that no other shop in Bardhaman or Calcutta sold such delicious ghugnee. Of course on days when we had evening duty in the factory, we remained deprived of its heavenly taste. On those days we were unable to leave the factory before 10 PM and by then the ghugnee would be all sold out.

We had even begged Jaguda several times to make it in larger quantities, but each time he had shaken his head and said – "No brother, that's not possible. Such items if cooked in large quantity do not taste as good. Besides, how can we rely on our customer's moods? Just because you have asked for that plate of ghugnee at this late hour tonight, what is the guarantee that you will come tomorrow also? For the sake of our business to prosper, its better that our stocks get finished quickly."

Incidentally, the mutton ghugnee in Jaguda's shop was known as *Pantar ghugnee*. We wonder whether there was anybody not only from Khepu, but from even within the seven or eight neighbouring villages who had not tasted the famous *pantar ghugnee* at least once?

After finishing our evening duties, we would often walk over to Jaguda's stall for a cup of tea. The tea was sweetened with molasses and cost only 12 paise per cup. Jaguda had informed everybody that he would not be able to serve sugar at times of such of high inflation, but the tea that he made with molasses and ginger was so delicious that after having tasted it once, it was impossible for anybody to stay away from it even for a day.

In fact, once we had even asked him whether he mixed something special in that tea, why else was it so addictive?

Jaguda would of course laugh and say, "Is it possible to get such drugs free of cost? Can I afford to become a pauper by mixing a costly drug in a cup of tea worth only 12 paise?"

One couldn't eat or drink here on credit. If anyone tended to linger for hours over just a cup of tea, then Jaguda would immediately raise his voice, and order his waitress, "Mano, go and clean that table." And that itself was enough of a hint for the customer to leave.

Of course, passers by from the road did not visit this stall too often. It was only on Saturdays and Tuesdays when the roadside bazars were held that such people came. Apart from that, it was basically the workers from our match factory who frequented the shop. The ten acres of land in the backyard also belonged to Jaguda, and he used it to grow vegetables like potatoes and peas. In the evenings, he generally slept in a room adjacent to the stall.

In the twenty years that we have been visiting the tea shop, we have seen it neither grow nor shrink. As far as we knew, Jaguda had not married. In fact, he didn't really have anyone to call his own except a widowed aunt who had arrived here some seven years back, along with her twelve year old daughter. Apparently, the old woman had met with bad times and lost all her land and property. Unable to sustain herself any longer, she had come and wept at Jaguda's feet asking for shelter for herself and her daughter. Jaguda hadn't thrown them out, in fact he had got them to work in his tea shop. Earlier, Jaguda himself would serve the tea the but now the young girl took over that duty. Her mother got busy with cleaning utensils, sweeping the floor and supervising the backyard. Indeed, it was after a long time that Jaguda found some free time for himself. At times he even joined his customers for a friendly chat over a cup of tea.

After a few years, Jaguda's aunt suddenly died of cholera, and some of us carried her body and cremated her on the bank of the river. The young girl, Manorama, had in the meantime learnt her work quite well. In fact she had already started making tea like Jaguda's, and to be honest, the mutton ghugnee that she prepared tasted even better. She was quite adept in handling money also. It seemed that Jaguda was quite relieved to leave the responsibility of running the shop in the young girl's hands.

Manorama wasn't really all that old, she must have been only fifteen or sixteen years of age then, but somehow she seemed much older. She was tall and well built and possibly a little overweight. She had a dark complexion and her face bore marks left by an attack of small pox she had suffered as a child. Her voice was rather manly and when she spoke, she didn't usually mince her words.

The fact that Jaguda and Manorama lived together in the same shop had attracted the attention of many curious people who didn't lose time in spreading a few scandalous stories about the two. To them, there was something definitely improper about Manorama spending the night with a man like Jaguda. So what if she was his aunt's daughter! Besides who knew whether the old lady had really been his Aunt!

Jaguda felt extremely hurt when such stories reached him. But he expressed his feelings only to some of his old customers like us. "Tell me," he said, "How can people think of such sinful things! Don't they realise that I have no interest in women – why else would I remain unmarried all these years? Shame on them, it's my own cousin and yet they are spreading such scandals about her?. Where should she be staying at night if not here? You know, I am ready to marry her off to anyone who is willing, even if that means my having to beg or borrow from others. Why don't you people too start looking around for a groom for her?"

But it wasn't easy to find a groom for Manorama. Who would be willing to marry a girl with such a burnt, pock marked face? Besides, where could one find a young man to match her hefty appearance?

Those of us – that is myself, Ratan, Paran and Jiten who visited Jaguda's shop regularly, knew that Jaguda wasn't really a bad man, and that he felt no attraction for the fairer sex. Why else had we not ever heard him utter even a single dirty word in all these years?

However, as the scandal started spreading further, more and more people began to throng the tea shop. In fact, at times even we couldn't find a place to sit! So what if Manorama didn't have a pretty face! Even the sight of those oversized breasts bursting at the seams, and her voluptuous hips were enough to attract many lustful eyes! Some customers even tried to linger on by repeatedly asking for tea! After all, the other two tea shops in the market didn't have a woman serving tea – did they?

But Jaguda himself was not pleased at this sudden increase in customers! Actually, he preferred only a few regular faces in his shop! In fact, whenever the new customers tended to raise their voices he would remind them that it was not a market place where they could shout as they pleased!

Anyway, things were going on somehow. One day, Jaguda did the most foolish thing on earth The first monsoon of the year had barely arrived when Jaguda suddenly died. Why didn't he think even for once, as to what would become of the young girl now?

I remember we had a night duty that day. It was about five thirty in the morning when a few of us along with Panchu, instead of Paran, walked over slowly to Jaguda's tea shop, as we usually did. There had been many occasions earlier also when we had found the shutters closed. On those days it was we who woke up Jaguda and got him to light the *chullah*. Strangely, he never expressed any dissatisfaction even if we landed up at such early hours. But that day when we arrived at the shop we found Manorama sitting and weeping in a corner. "*Dada*, oh *Dada*" she kept mourning and sobbing in a monotonous tone. We had never heard her cry earlier, in fact she had not wept so loudly even at her mother's deathbed! That is why we were surprised to hear her broken voice and loud wailings! We walked quietly to the next room and found Jaguda's body lying stiff on the floor, with his eyes wide open. We felt a shiver run through our back. Panchu bent down and touched him lightly. "It's frozen cold. He must have died long back." He whispered.

We noticed two pillows lying side by side on the bed – so Jaguda and Manorama must have been sharing the same bed. Manorama now sat weeping in one corner of the room, her clothes completely dishevelled. Unseen by others, I quickly pushed Maorama's pillow to one corner of the room. After all, people would be arriving soon, why give them a chance to wag their tongues?

As far as we knew, Jaguda hadn't been suffering from any disease. Why did he pass away so suddenly? People said that it was probably a heart attack. Apparently one could die of this very suddenly, even while lying in bed.

"Jaguda must have had a weak heart." "Panchu remarked. "There is a good homoeopathic cure for this. Oh, if I had only known a little earlier!" He repented.

Any way, all of us carried Jaguda's body to the crematorium and lit the pyre. Of course, all the while, we kept wondering silently as to what was going to become of the young girl now? In fact, that was what she herself was grieving about. "Oh Ma, where shall I now go, who shall I go to?" She kept repeating tearfully between sobs.

A few days passed by. We came to the tea shop everyday. Of course, there was no tea waiting for us, but how could we resist coming here? Hadn't this been our habit over the last twenty years?

In the end, we advised Manorama to re-open the shop once again.

"After all, you have to survive" We told her. "And this is the only thing you can depend on! Besides, this shop was Jaguda's heart and soul, he would never find eternal peace if this shop ever closed down."

After the sixth day, Manorama set aside her grief and re-opened the shop. Soon, customers started pouring in. It is true that life does not wait for anybody. Even the passing away of such a fun-loving, imposing personality like Jaguda didn't bring about any change, and life went on as usual.

But of course we had to appreciate Manorama's courage. She lived all alone in that lonely tea shop by the deserted field. She even slept in the room that Jaguda died in; obviously, she wasn't scared. We had suggested that she appoint an elderly maid who could help her with the house work, and also keep her company at night. But Manorama had refused saying that there was no need for that. After all, employing someone also meant an added expense for her!

Soon, a year passed by without even a burgler attempting to break into the house. Of course the petty thieves in our area are all of small stature, none of them were bold enough to break into the house of such an aggressive woman like Manorama. Indeed, she now appeared even more experienced and imposing than earlier. No one could make out her age by looking at her. We knew that she was twenty two years old, although she appeared at least ten years older!

Earlier, the shop did not have a signboard, now Manorama hung a placard that read – "JAGUDA'S TEA STALL." True, Jaguda was no more, but now his name had been immortalized with the shop. Manorama seemed to be running it quite efficiently. We were now her *de-facto* guardians. We were after all, the oldest customers and practically Jaguda's friends, so we had the right to that role. Manorama, on her part also, listened to us and accorded us that respect. She heeded our advice and suggestions. We – that is Tarun, Paran, Jiten and I came regularly to enquire about her well being. Sometimes Panchu also accompanied us.

We had three different duty shifts in our factory, – morning, afternoon and evening. Surprisingly, Manorama knew exactly which duty we had each week and she would keep waiting for us accordingly. On days when we had different duty hours, we wouldn't be able to visit the shop together. Even then, each of us would go and visit the shop at least once.

Manorama seemed quite capable of running the shop by herself. She made the tea, prepared the ghugnee and even cleared the tables herself. She had even added an extra item to her list of dishes – she had started serving omlettes. Also, next to the container of salted biscuits now stood an extra jar of slices of cake. We watched her growing efficiency with admiration!

One day, a customer tried to cheat her with a fake twenty-five bit coin. After having bought tea and a plate of ghugnee, he didn't ask for the eight paise change. Instead, he left the money in front of her and told her in rather a lordly manner, "Keep the change." But before he could even reach the door, Manorama had come running and held the man by the collar.

"Oh you goody goody man" She had taunted. "Did I serve you fake food that you are paying me fake money!"

Taken aback at her words the man had tried to feign innocence. "What did you say? A fake coin? Why I just got it from that cigarette shop at the street corner."

Manorama flung the coin onto the floor. "Then go and settle that with the cigarette shopkeeper. Just pay me proper money for the food that you have had here." She retorted.

To the man's embarrassment the coin fell on the floor without a thud. He quickly turned over his pocket and said, "But see, I don't have any more money with me."

"Is that so?" Manorama shouted back. "Didn't that dawn on you before you ordered your food?"

All this while, we had been watching the scene silently from a corner of the room. Of course we knew that if the man tried to create any further nuisance, we would catch him by the collar and teach him a lesson. After all, weren't we Manorama's guardians? What did he take Manorama to be – just a helpless, frail woman!

But we did not have to do anything. Manorama herself turned to the other customers and said, "Don't all of you know how hard I have been struggling to run this shop. I have never served anything stale – in fact I even threw away the two rotten eggs that I found in the basket yesterday, without worrying about the cost involved, and in return, are people going to cheat me like this? Tell me, is this fair?"

Those among the customers who were relatively new and had been coming here to see Manorama's physical stamina, reacted immediately. "Indeed, this is very wrong. We are sure that man has more money in his pocket."

Manorama was still holding onto the man's collar. The poor man was really in a desperate state. He seemed to be just a poor ordinary worker, but that was no excuse to forgive him.

"Take off his shirt, Mano" Paran ordered excitedly.

The man folded his hands and begged. "Please let me go. I have to attend a funeral today. I promise to come and pay the money tomorrow."

We laughed at the word – 'funeral'. "Well, why do you need to wear shoes at the funeral? Leave them here."

The man had a brand new pair of shoes on. Finally he had to leave his shoes behind before he was allowed to leave. Of course he never came back to reclaim his shoes. They remained in the shop until our own factory guard came and bought off the pair for a measly one and a half rupees!

On another occasion, a customer had walked in during the afternoon hours and misbehaved with Manorama. Apparently, while paying her money, he had stumbled indecently on her. I hadn't witnessed the scene myself, it was only Ratan from our group who was present in the shop that day. Seeing the man behave indecently, Ratan had immediately rushed to Mano's help. He was almost about to drag the man out by his collar, when Manorama had stopped him saying, "Just wait a minute Ratanda, let me teach this man a lesson he will remember his whole life." Saying this, she had dealt him such a hard punch, that his nose had started bleeding. Not surprising, was there anyone who could withstand a blow from that powerful fist?

Then she pushed him out, but not before she had spelt out her threats.

"If you ever dare to come this way again," She had warned. "I'll not spare a single bone in your body. I'll burn your face with a hot ladle from my kitchen. Did you hear?"

Since that incident, all doting, lustful young men had to remain contented only looking at her. No one dared to get closer to her, ever again.

There was something very common between Manorama and Jaguda. Like Jaguda, Manorama too did not make any attempt to increase profit by attracting more customers to her shop. She was more interested in running the shop peacefully with only a few select customers. All she wanted was a few genuine customers in return for the wholesome and tasty food that she served. On days when we had to do evening duties, we generally spent a longer time at the tea shop. Sometimes we would leave the factory at around eight thirty in the evening – about half an hour before schedule. In spite of being exhausted, we never felt like returning home. Our hearts longed to spend just a few hours together, sitting somewhere in private, and with a heart to heart conversation amongst ourselves.

Jaguda's shop was usually empty by that late hour. The last bus left at ten past nine, and the roads too seemed deserted. Of course, Manorama knew our duty hours and no matter how late we arrived, she would serve us tea as soon as we sat down. She would even clean the ash tray and bring it back to our table. After that she would sit at the counter and start counting the money that she had earned during the day.

She had a very strange style of singing. Her voice wasn't at all musical, it was like a man's. But, whenever she sang it was always in a very shrill tone – it sounded almost like a dog's wailing. And, it was always the same few lines of some strange song. We wondered where she had learnt that song from!

"How much did you earn today, Mano Didi?" Ratan asked.

"Between twenty seven and thirty paise. Not bad really." Manorama replied.

Even on days she earned less, she didn't seem remorseful or dissatisfied in the least. We heard her sing on those days as well. Sometimes, especially on Saturdays, she would save some ghugnee for us. Manorama knew that we had no duty on

Sundays, and therefore we would generally stay on and make merry on Saturday nights. We would walk into the stall and sit quietly at a corner table with a cup of tea each. We never spoke a word. It was only after the last customer left that we would break that silence. It was usually then that Ratan said, "Mano Didi, can you please get us four glasses?"

Those words were enough to annoy her. She would immediately walk over to our table, then standing with her hands on her hips, would say. "So you plan to drink all that rubbish again, is it?"

We would take out a bottle of some locally brewed liquor and tell her "But it's only locally made, and it will be finished in no time."

"Is that right? Are you sure you wont drink more?"

"No Didi, where would we find any more?"

Even though it was we who were her self-appointed guardians, it was she who now bossed over us. Of course we didn't tell her that all of us had a bottle each.

Manorama would come back with four glasses and then wrinkling her nose in distaste would say,

"My, what a terrible smell! What fun do you people get from drinking this?"

"Why don't you try drinking some! Then you might begin to enjoy it also." We teased.

"No, thank you. I don't need to feel happier. I am quite happy as it is."

It was always the same conversation every Saturday, but still we enjoyed it every time. Manorama would bring us four plates of ghugnee that she had possibly stored away for us during the day. We felt happy to notice that she warmed it up especially for us. Each time she went to the kitchen, we would quickly pour a little more wine into our glasses. Slowly, we could feel the headiness of the drink, our eyes would begin to turn red and beads of sweat appear on our foreheads. Paran would even begin to sing aloud, but Jiten stopped him promptly.

"Shut up, we don't want to hear you, we want Mano to sing now."

"Mano Didi, why don't you come a little closer." Ratan pleaded.

His pleading would be met only with a snub, "How much longer are you going to hang around here?" She would ask, gruffly.

"Oh we are almost through. We'll be leaving soon but until then, why don't you sit here and talk to us?"

Manorama pulled herself a chair but sat at a safe distance from our table so as to avoid the strong smell of the alcohol.

"Why don't you sing us that song?" Jiten said referring to the song with the strange words. Immediately Manorama began to hum, and after she had repeated the lines a number of times, we would start feeling somewhat enchanted. What a wonderful song it was, something no one else had heard!

Paran started drumming on the table, while Ratan wept in ecstacy.

"Mano Didi, can you dance?"

Manorama stood up and said, "Dance? Would you like to see me dance?"

And then closing her eyes, and spreading her arms on both sides she would begin to swirl, going round and round in circles almost as if she was playing the blindman's bluff. Wonder why she called it a dance! Whenever we asked her to dance, she would begin to swirl in that way. Truly, she seemed so beautiful then. So what if she was dark, and her face scarred by pock marks, it didn't even matter that her breasts and hips hung heavily like dumb bells, she still looked beautiful as she glided across the room. And as she danced, we would spread out in different corners of the room. It was like a game for the four of us.

"Mano, catch me if you can." We would shout out to her from a distance.

Swirling away, she would move in some direction and fall over one of us. We wouldn't make a sound, and she would have to tell which one of us it was. Without opening her eyes, she would glide her hands over the one she held on to, pull his ears, tug at his chin and then finally exclaim, "Why, this must be Baku'da, isn't it?"

Whenever she held on to me, and moved her hand over my face and arms, I felt so good! My body felt so soothed and relaxed that I prayed silently that she might not recognize me easily and hold on to me a little longer. At such moments, the others would stand at a little distance with envy in their eyes. But Manorama played this game only once each Saturday. So it was only one of us who would be lucky to have her close on those days.

Of course, each of us had a family waiting at home, a wife, a son, an old mother, a leaking roof above our head, worm-eaten vegetables, and a life full of unsatisfied need. The minute we stepped into our house, we would hear complaints and see sulking wives and mothers. But at this special moment every Saturday night, we would become oblivious of everything. At that moment, it was only the four of us and Manorama.

We knew that other young men liked to spend their money on movies watching heros and heroines clinging to each other on screen, but we wondered what joy they found in such entertainment! The cinema hall in our locality changed movies twice a week. But we never went there. After all we had our own Manorama, didn't we?

When it was almost eleven at night, Mano said, "Arent you people going home tonight? If you stay back longer, your wives will surely thrash you."

We laughed aloud at her words. Of course we knew that Manorama would start telling her story now – a story that she repeated every Saturday. Apparently, for some time her family had lived in one of her uncle's house in Burdwan, where a man and his wife lived as tenants upstairs. Every night the man would return home drunk and while entering would say, "Never again! I'll never touch a drink again." Hearing those words his wife would come running and thrash him hard, disturbing the entire neighbourhood.

Once this story came to an end, we would roll with laughter. "Stop Manodidi, please" Jiten would say clutching to his stomach. "Don't tell us about such gentlemen who not only support their wives, but even withstand a beating from them. Its only men from the upper class who can put up with such things. But tell us, if someone like us had married you, would you have beaten him?"

"Of course I would have beaten the life out of him." Mano replied.

"Thank God that I didn't marry you. I am sure I would have been dead if you ever hit me with that hand of yours." Ratan teased.

Ratan often came up with naughty ideas. He would pretend that his foot had gone to sleep and would request Manorama to come and help him get up. But as soon as she tried to pull him up, he would twine his arms around her neck like a patient holding on to a nurse. Of course we could see through this prank of his!

And then Jiten would say "But all of us suffer from pins and needles. Mano will surely help us, won't she?"

It wasn't difficult for Mano to see through our game and guess our real intentions.

"You are all like overgrown children. Come on now, scoot. I'll push you out if you don't!" She said in mock threat.

That was actually as far as we would go with her. We never crossed that limit. It was time to go home now. After all we had a household, a house that was full of wants. After we walked out, Manorama pulled down the shutters for the day.

As we walked back together, Ratan suddenly said, "Our Mano is such a dear girl."

That is just what the rest of us were thinking also.

"Yes, she's such a wonderful girl, but unfortunately she couldn't find a groom for herself. Will she have to suffer like this all her life?" Of course, we had tried to find a groom for her, but couldn't get anyone suitable.

Ratan was now rather high. "If only I was not married already," he sobbed," I would certainly have married Manorama myself. And then I would have enjoyed her beatings as well."

Suddenly he stopped and looked at us. We looked back at him angrily. Hadn't we all committed a similar blunder already? Didn't we all have a nagging and prickly wife at home? Wouldn't we have been happier if we had married Manorama? But then, Manorama would have belonged to only the person who married her and deprived the others of her companionship. Could we still have played this game that we played on Saturday nights? No, it's much better that we are all married already. None of us can marry Manorama now. And that is why she could belong to all of us. Wasn't that the reason why we didn't bring Panchu here with us?

All of a sudden, five people from our factory were laid off. True, none from among us were in that list but we heard that there would be more such lay-offs. Who knew on whose head the axe would fall next! We lived in constant fear. The market scene was very bad, Apparently, cheaper matches from the south had flooded the market!

We left the factory each day with a bitter taste in our mouths. Who knew what notice we would find the next day! Moreover, some even feared a total lock-out!

We arrived at Jaguda's shop with drawn faces! In the meantime, Manorama had been working hard to set up the shop well. Now she was even thinking of replacing the old tables and chairs with new ones! Of course, we tried to advise her in a cool manner.

"Listen, these are not good times." We told her. "Its better to keep your money in hand."

"Why do you sit with such glum faces nowadays? Don't you find the tea tasty any more?" She asked.

"Of course not", we reply in protest. Wasn't her tea getting sweeter by the day?

We never ran up a credit in Manorama' shop, This was a tradition that we had followed right from Jaguda's time. Somehow we all felt that loans always multiplied, and finally never got paid. It also invariably led to bad relations with the shop owners. Even though we were her guardians, could anyone ever accuse us of having eaten anything on loan here! In fact, on days we had no money, we never came here.

But we all knew that even if one of us could not visit her, someone else would come and enquire of her well being. Of course none of us stayed away from the Saturday meet. We had already bribed the factory foreman to ensure that we were never given a night duty on Saturday.

Each time we took out our bottle of local liquor on Saturdays, Manorama would first scold us, but we knew that she enjoyed this special – session on Saturdays as much as we did. It was her only recreation after a week of hard work. The joy that she experienced in playing with us, was after all, the only happy moment in her life

One Saturday, we were waiting impatiently for the last customer to leave. But the man concerned didn't seem as if he would ever move. He kept sitting in a corner resting his chin on his palm, as if absorbed in deep thought. He was a tall and thin man, dressed in clean clothes. We hadn't seen him earlier. At first we had thought he sat there to eye Manorama greedily, but we realised now that it was not so. His eyes were focussed on the wall and he did not see anything else.

It was not our habit to drive away a customer unless he had

committed an offence. If people wished to sit for a little longer, they could do so, but this man had been sitting for hours over just a cup of tea!

Ratan coughed aloud and asked, "What is the time now!"

"It's past nine" Paran replied.

"Then the last bus should be leaving any moment now." Jiten added. We hoped that these words would bring the man to his senses and he would get up to leave. After all, he seemed to have come from a different place, how would he return home if he missed the last bus?

But our words seemed to have no effect on the man. Instead of leaving, he rested his head on the table. We looked at each other – wondering what was going on. We signalled to Manorama and she went and stood in front of the man. Then, in that rasping voice of hers she said, "Won't you drink your tea? It seems to have got cold long time back."

The man looked at Manorama without saying anything.

"I shall be closing my shop now". Manorama announced.

This time the man spoke. "I'll keep resting on this table – just for the night." He said, uttering each word slowly.

What was he saying! His intentions didn't seem good! His voice sounded quite effusive. No, he wouldn't be allowed to play the fool here! Of course he didn't know that we – Manorama's guardians were present in the room.

Ratan walked up to the man and said, "Listen Sir, just get up, will you? This is not a place for sleeping!"

"Only for the night, I'll stay here only for the night. I am ready to pay."

Ratan was about to hit the man now. "If you need to sleep, why don't you go to a hotel, why are you hanging around here?"

"Is there a hotel nearby?"

"Yes, Hotel Annapurna is near the market. You can go there right away."

"Alright, I'll go. Could you just help me get up? I am unable to stand up on my own."

Ratan came forward and held the man by his arms. "My goodness!" He exclaimed, as soon as he touched him. Turning towards me, he said – "Come here quickly". And then as soon as I reached him, said, "Just see, if you can make out what's wrong with him!"

By this time, the man had laid his head back on the table. Like Ratan, I too was taken aback as I touched him. His body felt extremely hot, it was almost burning.

"He seems to be running high fever." I said.

This time the man raised his blood-red eyes at me and said, "Just lift me a little please, and then I will be able to find my way alright."

The language he used was not quite like our's. There was a definite urban touch to his words.

I watched him closely. He had very handsome features and looked almost like a film star. Why had a man of his class suddenly come to a place like this?

This time, Ratan and I held the man by his arms and helped him to his feet. The man was staggering like a drunkard.

"What has happened to you?"

"I have a splitting headache." He said wearily.

"Maybe he has malaria." Jatin shouted from across the room.

"How can you possibly leave in this condition? You might even fall down any moment! Where do you live?"

"Somewhere very far from here."

"From where did you come to this shop?"

The man didn't reply, he looked up wearily and again said, "Please help me only up to the road."

All this while Manorama had been watching this scene from a little distance away, standing with her hands on her hips. This time it was she who spoke aloud." Are you all sure it's fever and not sheer drunkenness?"

"No that wouldn't have made the body so warm."

"Well, will he be able to walk then?" She asked again.

"No, Possibly not."

"Then just put him down on that table." She said.

I too had been thinking of doing the same. After all there was no sense in leaving a sick man on the road. One could easily make out that he was from a well to do family. Why on earth had he come here of all places?

We laid the man back on the table. It would be nice if we could have called a doctor right away, but where would we find one at this late hour?

"Won't you take some medicine?" I asked the man.

"No that will not be necessary, I will be alright by tomorrow."

"Shall I wash his head with cold water?" Manorama asked.

"Yes, why not!" We said in chorus.

Manorama left the room and after a while returned with a

bucket that she used for scrubbing the floor, and a mug in her hand. She had barely begun to pour the water on the man's head when she suddenly exclaimed, "Oh my, he has fainted already! Ratanda, see there's such a swelling on his right heel, something seems wrong here! Could it be a snake bite or something?" She asked anxiously.

"No, that's impossible. Could anybody talk for so long after being bitten by a snake?"

"It could be just ordinary fever! Has he really fainted? let me see." Ratan tried to move the body but without much success. The man had fainted alright. Still, Manorama kept washing his head with cold water.

In the midst of all this, we realised that we hadn't been able to take out our bottles of liquor yet. It was growing late now, and we had to return home.

Paran just couldn't hold on to his patience any longer. "Mano" He said, "Come and give us our glasses please, we just can't wait any more."

But even though we finally managed to drink that night, we didn't enjoy ourselves as much as we usually did. Manorama did not sing her usual song either. We couldn't ask her to dance. After all there was a stranger in the room. How could we play that game of ours in his presence! That game that we played every Saturday night was not known to any else in the world! It was a moment when we remained completely dissociated from the outside world, it was a time only for the four of us and of course Manorama. Why did this stranger from nowhere have to come here and spoil all the fun? If instead of him, it had been a dacoit, then we could have fought with all our might to keep him away from her. But here was a sick man, how could we throw him onto the street? We couldn't object even if Manorama wanted to wash his head, could we?

We spent a long time sitting with sullen faces. It was time to leave now. Each one of us went and touched the man's forehead, we needed to know whether the he was really sick. If he had been feigning illness all along, we would kick him out at this very minute!

No, we found his skin still very warm, as if on fire. He was still unconscious. After all no one could wilfully raise the temperature of his own body, could he?

Seeing us preparing to leave, Manorama asked, "Will he just keep lying like that? Will he not eat anything tonight?"

"He doesn't even have the strength to eat." Ratan replied.

"But Ratanda, what if he dies?"

"Come on, is it so easy to die just like that? Nobody dies of fever. Let him keep resting for now. You can drive him out tomorrow morning."

As soon as we walked out, Manorama closed the shutters. All of us felt somewhat uneasy, we were her guardians and yet we had left her with a total stranger. But what else could we have done?

After a while, Jiten said, "Wonder who that man is? Could he be a thief or something like that?"

"He didn't seem like one." Paran remarked.

– "Come on, can you make out what people are like from their appearances? After all, thieves in big cities look like gentlemen, don't they?"

"But what would a thief from the city come to steal from Jaguda's shop?"

"Could he be a political prisoner? Maybe he has escaped from a jail. Who knows?"

"The man didn't tell us his name or address. Where could he be from?"

"Hope it will not lead to the police getting involved!"

Ratan suddenly halted, "Maybe one of us should have stayed back with Manorama tonight." He said, in a thoughtful tone. "In case there is any kind of danger!"

The three of us looked at him, piercingly. Ratan was speaking selfishly. Didn't each of us also wish the same? Didn't we want to stand by Manorama in her time of trouble? But we also knew that if any of us stayed back the night with her, he would play that game all by himself, and that would make the other three green with envy.

Seeing our piercing looks, Ratan felt somewhat bewildered. Starting to walk again he said, "Would my wife excuse me if I didn't return home tonight? She would possibly come running to drag me back. She knows quite well where we usually spend our Saturday evenings!"

All of us heaved a sigh of relief. We had wives and children at home. There was no need to add to our existing troubles! Staying back the night with Manorama would definitely spell trouble for us at home. Each of us kept an eye on the other three to see if anyone visited her at night. After all Manorama didn't belong exclusively to any one of us.

None of us had a duty that following Sunday. I walked over

to Jaguda's shop on my way to the morning market. Soon the other three also arrived, as if we had pre-planned it.

No other customer had come for tea as yet. It was only the four of us. Even the last night's stranger was not resting on the table where we had left him.

We called out to Manorama, but there was no response. We walked to the back of the shop and peeped into the kitchen. On other days, the *chullah* would generally be lit by this time, but today we found Manorama lying on the floor, still asleep. Hearing us call out again, she sat up quickly, and rubbed her eyes. "Oh you have come already!"

"Why are you sleeping here?" We asked her.

"I wasn't sleeping, I was just resting a bit. After all I couldn't sleep a wink last night. I felt very scared."

We were amazed! Manorama feeling scared! We had never heard her say any such thing earlier. So we said, "Why Mano Didi, why did you feel scared?"

Tightening the end of her saree around her waist, Manorama said, "Wouldn't I? You know that man was making such rattling sounds – his chest probably, and he moaned all night, I feared that he might die any moment! How could you leave me with such a man? Didn't you worry about me at all?"

"Of course Mano, its only you we thought of all night. Even with our sickly wives and cranky kids by our side, we only thought of you. After all, what else do we have apart from you? But of course there was no other way out for us. None of us could spend the night alone with you, even if we wished to. Anyway, where did that man go? Has he left?"

"Where can he go? He must be lying in my room still."

"What? In your room? How did he go there, did he walk on his own? Then he must be a very bad man."

"Why would he go on his own? Did he have that much strength left? He was making such rattling sounds last night, and I was scared that he might fall off the table any moment and collapse. In that case, wouldn't the police come and arrest me!"

We went and peeped into Manorama's room. We found the man lying in just the same way as Jaguda had, when he had lain dead on that bed! We felt a shiver going through our hearts! Had the man really died?

But the very next instant, we knew he hadn't. His heart was heaving. A wet cloth was placed on his forehead. We found that Manorama had covered him with a sheet.

Apparently she had carried him on her own from the table. Of course she was strong enough to do so. But, somehow, that man looked out of place here. It seemed as if a prince had suddenly walked in to a poor household and fallen asleep.

But how long could he keep on sleeping here? After all, people would start to come any moment. And if they got to know of his presence, then it wouldn't take long for all kinds of rumours to start flying!

All of us crowded near the door, unable to decide who should call the man first. We just kept looking at each other's face. It was at this time that the man suddenly woke up. With his eyes opened wide, he said, "Where am I?"

"You are ill." Ratan said.

"Who are you all?"

"It was we who laid you down on the table yesterday, don't you remember?"

"Oh yes, but isn't this a bed?"

"Yes, it is. It is the tea shop owner's bed."

Ratan touched the man's forehead and said – "You seem to be having fever still. In that case, we need to call a doctor. Will you be able to go to a hospital?"

"That won't be necessary." The man said. "As soon as I feel a little better, I'll leave on my own. You don't need to tell anyone that I am here."

"Why? Who are you anyway?"

The man folded his hands and said, "Believe me, I am not a bad man. I just cannot disclose my identity right now."

We hate to see any man from the upper strata of society talk to us with folded hands. We have seen enough of all this play-acting, folding hands when necessary and then threatening at other times. But we couldn't tell him anything directly. The way he was talking, it was clear that he was in great pain. It seemed there was more trouble ahead for us.

I hadn't yet bought the groceries I was supposed to. I couldn't delay any more, after all this was the only day in the week when I went to the market myself.

We came outside and found that Manorama had already lit the *chullah*. She was heating the milk now. Seeing us, she said "Just wait a while, will you. The tea will be made soon. Anyway, how did you find him to be?"

"Well, he still seems to have high fever."

"He hadn't eaten last night. Maybe I could offer him some warm milk now, shall I?"

"Yes, why don't you."

We finished our tea and left immediately. We couldn't visit the shop again that day. Actually, when the factory remains closed, its' not possible for us to come so far frequently. In fact that is why, there are such few customers in this shop on Sundays.

Even after three days had passed by, the man couldn't leave. Along with fever, he developed unbearable pain in his head and chest. Ratan thought that he had pneumonia while Jiten said it was tuberculosis. Was it right for Manorama to remain close to such infectious diseases anyway? But Manorama was nursing him day and night. She had lost her concern for running the shop, customers had to leave without getting even a cup of tea. Not only that, she didn't pay any attention even to us who were her guardians after all. Whenever we tried to tell her anything, she would say. "But then can I let the man just die? After all he is a gentleman! Has he come to die in my house? Don't you feel any sympathy for him?"

Ratan had secretly brought her some ayurvedic medicine. He had tried to keep it a secret from us. But he couldn't escape our eyes! On being exposed, he said, "Don't you understand, the quicker he recovers, the better for us. Otherwise, the way Manorama has been behaving of late, I am afraid the shop might even close down!

"I heard some people at the road crossing talking about some man who is apparently hiding in Jaguda's shop. It'll be dangerous if this news spreads further!"

We shook our heads gravely. True, it really meant trouble. The man too did not want to disclose his own identity. Of course, we wanted to protect Manorama from any kind of trouble, but how could we save her from this one?

By the fifth day, the stranger who had by now recovered somewhat, sat up on the bed. In the meantime, Manorama had kept her shop closed for the last two days. People were told that she was unwell, although we, her five friends knew the truth. We visited her secretly in the evening to find out the news, but left without even a cup of tea. Actually, Manorama forgot to offer us any.

We peeped through the door, and found the man sitting up on the bed. Manorama was sitting in a corner of the room and looking at him steadfastly. The man looked at us and said, "Come in. It seems I have been saved this one time."

We stepped in and stood against the wall. There was a suppressed joy in our hearts. So, the man would be leaving finally. And with a Saturday just round the corner, we would get back Manorama to ourselves again, just as before.

The man turned towards Manorama and said, "It's her constant care and nursing that saved me. She is really a very kind woman, after all, I was only a stranger, an unknown person!"

This was the first time that we heard someone else describe Manorama as a kind person. People generally knew her to be a very angry and dominating woman. Of course we knew what she was truly like. Had she not been kind, would she have helped us back on our feet whenever we asked her?

"I don't know how I shall repay her. I have no money with me ..." The man said ruefully.

Manorama cut in loudly, "Let it be, you don't have to worry about repaying anything now. You've not even got back your strength fully yet ..."

"But I don't ever forget favours done to me. I'll surely return some day. If I live ..."

"That's all in the future. For the present, I am not letting you go now. First, you should eat properly and regain your strength."

"That's not a bad idea. I could eat well and gain strength and then work here as a tea boy. I could carry the tea to the tables, wash the dishes ..."

The next day we found the shop open but there was not a single customer around. Manorama was sitting at the counter with a sullen face. She looked at us, but didn't say a word.

"Where did that man go?" We asked her.

Maorama gestured silently.

"What happened Mano Didi? what happened?"

This time she raised her voice. "Gone, he has gone."

We felt like dancing in joy. Thank God, it was good riddance to bad rubbish!

"Remember, he was even talking about working as a tea boy here. Such ostentatious words really! could he have worked as a tea boy with his princely look?"

"Anyway, when and how did he go?"

"Did he even tell me that? He didn't give me even the slightest hint. I had left him for a while – and gone to bathe in the pond nearby. When I came back, I found he was gone. He couldn't even walk properly, how did go?"

"He must have had bad intentions. Are you sure he didn't steal anything?"

"Oh Manodidi, are you sure he didn't steal a thing or two?" We repeated.

"Will you be quiet. I am not feeling well. And what great treasures do I have that he would steal?"

We fell silent.

After a few days, it was Saturday again. But Manorama did not sing her song. She did not dance. We did not play our usual game. Manorama was no longer the same, she did not pay us any attention. She just kept sitting by herself. Days passed like this. We realised that even if that man had not stolen anything from the shop, he had taken away her heart completely. We never again got to know what that heart was really like.

One day, Ratan braced himself and said, "How many more days will you keep sitting like this, fretting over why that man left? Can't you see, the shop is almost closing down!"

Manorama's eyes filled with tears. "But didn't he say that he would come back some day?"

She asked, slowly.

Of course those were just the false words of city-bred people. What worth did they have anyway? How could we possibly make Manorama realise that?.

If we could, we would have dragged the man back. But where could we find him now? Our factory could face a lock-out any time, so we didn't dare to stay away from work even for a day.

But we felt furious inside. We had nothing else, no other joy. Our lives are pitted with wants. We have no film heroes or heroines to idolise. We don't need to know anything about the outside world, either. All we had was Manorama, but that man with the princely look, that man from the city – they have so many sources of entertainment and joyous occasions in their lives. When then still, did he have to steal our Manorama's heart for ever?

Shahjehan and his own Battalion
Shahjahan O tar Nijashwa Bahini

One day, a row broke out suddenly in the Gajipur market. The sweet potato and pumpkin sellers often fought with each other over a place to sit, and sometimes their fights even turned violent. That day, the altercation wasn't all that serious, it seemed to have more smoke than fire. People screamed, abused and shoved each other around. A few had even raised their sticks, but they all came down only on one head. Whose could it be but Haju's? He sold neither potatoes nor pumpkins, he was just a good-for-nothing fellow.

The sight of blood streaming down Haju's face sent a wave of panic among both the groups. They stopped fighting immediately and fell over him showering words of sympathy. Even though the sudden blows had knocked him down, Haju hadn't made a sound. With his hands pressed against his bleeding head, he looked around like a frightened animal, as if it had all been his fault. Indeed it was, for soon after their kinds words came to an end, people started blaming him for what had happened.

"Why did you have to come in between, you fool?" They charged.

But this had always been Haju's fate. Somehow he always got drawn into dangerous situations. Wasn't it only sometime back that an angry bull had attacked him in the same market? That day too, it was only he who had got badly mauled while no one else had got hurt. On another occasion, he had been bitten by a poisonous snake while trying to pluck water-weeds from a pond. In fact that was the first time that someone from Gajipur had got bitten by a snake.

But why did Haju roam around the market? After all, he was neither a seller nor a buyer. With his tall frame clad in a vest and a green and black striped lungi wrapped around his waist, he loitered around the market, mindlessly. Actually, it was his straight and lean appearance that made his limbs seem longer and more haggard looking. Added to that, he shaved once a week or ten days. Sometimes he would sit down and gaze at faces that passed by, faces which were both familiar and unfamiliar, but there wasn't any pleading or beggary in his eyes then; it was rather the opposite. He seemed as if he was totally indifferent to life and his own surroundings.

The Gajipur market was not known to be a good place. With the huge transaction of money that was carried out there, it naturally attracted the attention of several hawks. There were also enough people who were ready to incite at the slightest opportunity, a riot between Hindus and Muslims. Even though the shop keepers were all Hindus, the money lenders were

Muslims, and though the sitting MLA, Sheikh Anwar Ali was a Muslim, the previous one – Vishnu Sikdar still had a lot of power over the local people. Things therefore seemed to be somewhat on a balance here, but the balance was like a very fine thread that could snap any moment.

It was really only the very devious who could get their way here. One had to be strong either in words, money or musclepower. But Haju had none of these. In fact he seemed to lack sensitivity of any kind. He didn't know how to ask from others or even give them anything. When he was younger, he used to be often seen standing under a palm tree in a deserted field, gazing at the sky – as if trying to search for something in the crimson-coloured rays of the setting sun. Those who saw him then, often wondered whether he would turn into a *fakir* some day.

But ever since he had fallen off that tree accidentally, he no longer stood there. Instead, he now watched the reflection of the setting sun in the waters of the canal.

Seeing Haju sitting there with his bleeding head in his hands, his uncle's friend Mojammal rushed forward with an ointment made out of some flower juice. After rubbing the paste on the wound, he handed him a *bidi* and said – "Haju do you think you will be able to recognize the man who beat you?"

"No, Mojammal Chacha." Haju said, shaking his head.

Mojammal looked at him with contempt and said – "Who says you are worthless? Wasn't it only because you got beaten, that those people stopped fighting!" Then he suddenly lowered his tone and said – "Listen Haju, it was I who beat you. Now go home, run."

Haju lit the bidi and began to walk slowly homeward. Mojammal's words hadn't made any impact. His head was still throbbing with pain, a streak of blood had trickled down his shoulders and stained a part of his vest at the back. After crossing the canal which had dried up, he continued to walk slowly through the field. Nobody had ever seen him walk fast. In fact everything in his life moved at a very slow pace. But what could he do, after all it was God who had created him like this! So he trudged back home, watching his own shadow fall in the afternoon sun.

Even though Haju was born in a Muslim family, he was like an obstinate Hindu, one who couldn't be put to any use. He could neither work in the fields, nor do any work in the house — an inability for which he had been rebuked several times in the past, by his father and uncle. But eventually they had all given up. It wasn't that Haju wanted to play truant at work, he was absolutely incapable of doing anything. Even if someone asked him to do as much as remove the weeds from the field, he would keep sitting quietly with a sickle in hand, staring at the weeds as if he was meditating seriously. Actually, he would be thinking of nothing then, his mind a complete blank.

Like everybody else, Haju too had been married off at the right age. He had four children now, but he just couldn't bring himself to be a proper husband or a father. His sons didn't obey him, in fact they were rather insolent. His wife too was an extremely sharp-tongued woman, she continued clamouring the whole day until she frothed at the mouth, but even then, it didnt seem to have any effect on Haju. He neither flared up nor swung into action. He continued to remain just as indifferent as before.

Before entering his house, Haju went to wash his feet in the nearby pond. He kept scrubbing his heels and toes slowly, as if he had all the time in the world. Indeed, once he reached his house, he would keep sitting in the the verandah till it grew dark and his food was served. That was the only thing he liked, he loved to eat, though it was true that of late, he hadn't been getting his meals regularly All these years, as a member of a large joint family, he had somehow managed to get his meals alright. His own *amma*, like all other mothers with a weak child, had always nourished a special concern for this useless son of hers. But she had died last year and his father had died even earlier. With both the parents gone, his elder brother had moved away from the joint family and set up his own establishment. In fact, Haju was not even aware of how the family was being run now.

It was his wife Sayeeda who first noticed the wound on his head.

"Is that blood on your head?" She asked.

"Yes." Haju replied.

"How did you get that cut? Where did you fall down again?" she asked, coming closer. Her voice kept rising with every step. She had a tight, streamlined body, it didn't seem that she was already a mother of four. She had to work hard the whole day doing the job of two men. Besides, she had a very sharp tongue also. Haju's eldest son was only thirteen years old but he had already learnt to speak like a shrewd man. He worked as a cow-herd in some house nearby. Hearing his mother's voice, he came and joined her in the verbal attack on his father. Soon, the others in the family also came and crowded around.

Of course Haju never felt disturbed in any kind of way. He knew that this day would turn out like any other. People would keep scolding and shouting at him, and after a while they would all quieten down. The darkness outside would gradually deepen, and night birds and wolves would begin to be heard in the distance, just like every night. But little did Haju know then that a big change was soon to enter his life.

Within a short time, everybody came to know that Haju hadn't really cut his head in a fall, someone had actually hit him with a stick. This sudden news brought out different reactions from different people – some were angry, others felt sad. Everybody knew that a thoroughly innocent and simple man like Haju could never do something that warranted a beating. And yet, life was so strange that it was only people like Haju who always got punished.

Haju stood quietly, a few strands of hair stuck to his head with blood. His head was still throbbing. He heard the people around but there was no change of expression on his face. He had no anger or complaint against anybody. "I am not sure how exactly I got hurt." He mumbled. "I felt a blow on my head, and I think I fell. But it didn't really hurt all that much, there was only a little blood!"

Eklas, Sayeeda's elder brother had just arrived in this house and now along with the others in the family, he too came to know about the incident at the market. Eklas himself had suffered and learnt a lot in life, he knew the cost of innocence in the present times. His own home was just two villages away from this place, and even though he had been living in the city for many years now, he still kept news of what went on in the villages. His urbanised ears had not failed to hear the sound of a crash in the rural world.

Eklas was his way to the city, when he decided to rest a while at his sister's place. After hearing everything, he proposed that Haju come with him. Maybe, he would be able to train him and make him self-supporting.

At first nobody paid any heed to Eklas's words. After all, wasn't it certain that if a useless and idiotic fellow like Haju moved to a city, he would get run over by a car within the very first day or two? And how could he ever make a living? What work could he do? If he couldn't make do in the villages, what would he do in a city where people were so ruthlessly competitive?

But Eklas brushed off all these and said, "Don't we know that when a fire breaks out in a house, even the most ignorant member of the family tries to save his own life. There are so many such fires burning in the city. It is that fire which will ultimately teach him to survive. See, in spite of living so many years in a village, he hasn't been able to make any money, where as in a city, he would, if nothing else, at least be able to tie *bidis* and earn a few rupees for himself. Nobody goes hungry in a city!"

All the while that Eklas spoke, Haju continued to gaze at him in rapt attention. He didn't know what a city was! He had never stepped outside the neighbourhood of these 8-10 villages that was bounded by Munshidanga on one side and Sulemanpur on the other. Yet when Eklas said, "Haju, you'll come with me, won't you?" he immediately nodded his head and said, "Yes."

The journey to the city was put off till the next day. Early next morning, Haju set out with Eklas, with a couple of bags in his hand. He looked rather pleased. Before stepping out of the house, Eklas turned to Sayeeda and said, "Don't worry, I'll take care! Just wait and see, he will surely send you some money in a month or two!"

They would have to walk seven miles before taking the bus at Aranghata. A new road had been constructed with the mud dug out from the canal. It was a beautiful morning. The sun wasn't all that warm, and a cool breeze blew. Haju walked on, watching his own reflection in the canal. Eklas was very fond of talking and he kept jabbering endlessly, but not much of it made any sense to Haju! It seemed as if he had discovered for the first time how beautiful the sky looked in the flowing waters!

When they had almost reached Sulemanpur, Eklas suddenly stopped and exclaimed "What on earth is that! Haju, look at the field on your right!"

A procession of people carrying banners was approaching this side. There were about a hundred and fifty people at least, and they were raising some slogans. Again there were a number of people waving flags, sticks and axes on this side of the canal also.

"Are they planning on a *kajia* here today? Come on Haju, let's move fast. Hope we don't get caught up in this!"

But of course, Haju couldn't walk fast, he kept staring at the procession, in silent amazement. The procession was just beginning to leave the field and step on to the embankment, it's long serpentine line of people moving slowly. There was a small bamboo bridge nearby which they would have to cross before reaching the field on the other side. Once there, a scuffle between the two groups was imminent.

Haju hadn't seen that bridge on his last trip to Sulemanpur. Who had built it? Had they made it only for this fight?

After taking a few hurried step Eklas looked back and found Haju standing still, with his eyes glued in the direction of the procession. He seemed to observe everything in life with such intense attention!

By now, the voices of the people in the procession and those waiting on the field on the other side had reached a peak.

Eklas walked back a few steps, and pulled Haju by the hand. "What are you gaping at, idiot? Would you like to get thrashed again? Come on, hurry!"

He dragged Haju almost all the way until they had crossed Sulemanpur and arrived near Ratan Agarwal's cold storage. Then panting heavily, the two men paused a while to regain their breath.

After a while Eklas said, "From what we saw today, at least five or seven people must be lying dead there by now."

Immediately, a sight of seven bodies lying on their faces, sides and back, floated before Haju's eyes. The land which was to have borne a shining crop now lay smeared with blood.

"Do you know why human beings kill each other?" Eklas asked.

Sayeda often said that whenever Haju meditated seriously, his eyes took on a bovine look. And that is exactly how he looked now. He looked up, a little startled at Eklas's question." I don't understand all that, Eklas *Bhai*." He said.

"Why can't you understand? One could, if one tried a bit."

"I do try, but when I was young, the senior Mullah had told

me that I had worms in my head, and that is why I can't understand anything!"

"Rubbish! People kill each other only to save their own lives. If anyone ever comes to hit you, you should hit him first. Otherwise, you'll not be able to survive."

"But I don't hit anyone; why do people still hit me?"

"That's because you have always been like a stupid ass. Come on, I'll make a man out of you in the city."

They drank water from the tube-well in front of the cold storage and cooled themselves before resuming their walk.

The house that Eklas lived in Calcutta was a two-floor building in Darga lane, near Moulali. It was a kind of a hostel shared by twelve others who lived with their families. All of them left for work early and returned home after it was dark.

Of course, it wouldn't be difficult to feed one more mouth from the collective food cooked for the twelve families, but still Haju would need to do something in return. At first he was asked to cook. But Haju didn't know how to cook, he not only ended up burning the rice but burnt his own hand as well. He kept staring at the fire burning in the *chullah*, as if that too was something worth seeing.

After that he was given the charge of washing clothes and utensils. But when people returned from work in the evening, they found Haju sitting amidst a pile of wet clothes and heaped up un-washed utensils, as if totally mesmerised by the sight and sound of water flowing from the tap.

Saifulla, a patron of this house was rather a serious man working at the Small Causes court. It was difficult for him to withstand such a sight at the end of a hard day's work. Livid with fury, he charged into the room and pulled up Haju by his ears.

"Rascal, wicked!" He shouted, as he slapped him hard.

Eklas who was standing close by, was quick to react. "I have brought him here to make a man out of him." He said in a rather serious tone. "Of course he will have to endure at least a beating or two!"

So, Haju became more of a man indeed! That evening, he had to clean all the utensils and wash all the clothes as well. Both Eklas and Saifulla kept guard all along, and whenever his hands slowed down, they kicked him hard on his back.

Of course, Haju didn't feel hurt at this. He was really getting to like this place. Within a few days he began to mingle well the people and their ways. All the fourteen members of the hostel took turns to 'train' him and also beat him hard whenever he failed. Among them, were three or four boys who were only as old as his son. Even they didn't hesitate to hit him, but Haju seemed to like it.

In the lonely afternoon hours, when the house was almost empty, Haju sat on the open balcony outside, watching a variety of people and hawkers go by. From a mosque nearby, one could hear the *ajan* every morning and evening. Haju had never heard an *ajan* on a microphonre earlier, and the tune simply enchanted him. He felt as if God's own voice was floating down from the Heavens.

And once he himself sat down to say his *namaz*, he wouldn't get up easily. He would keep staring at the floor-in fact he could spend hours just sitting like that. Finally it would be Nayeem and Kader who would pull him back to his feet again!

Eklas had promised his sister that he would find Haju a way of earning. After all, he wouldn't be able to make much of his life if he continued to live on other people's charity. So he arranged for Haju to work with a group of people who tied *bidis* in a slum nearby. It was an easy job that didn't require running around, and it didn't involve any physical strain either. There was no obeying orders from a boss. All he had to do was to stretch out his legs somewhere, rest a basket of raw materials on his lap and keep tying 'bidis', one after another. For every thousand *bidis* that he tied, he would be paid six rupees. There were some who even made as many as a thousand and five hundred or two thousand daily. Anyway, Haju could start with a thousand first. If not thousand, at least five hundred.

On the first day, Haju made only five bidis and the next day he made seven. The other craftsmen began to laugh at him. "Oh *Mia*, did you fall asleep?" They kept taunting him from different corners of the room

But Haju hadn't fallen asleep. The truth was that he just couldn't take his eyes off the raw materials with which the *bidis* were to be made. The look and aroma of the mixture simply enchanted him, and that is what slowed him down. In spite of being rebuked and ridiculed, Haju just couldn't make more than ten bidis a day. Finally one day, the bidi-owner called Eklas and said, "It is impossible to keep this man. He just sits with a full basket uselessly. What can I pay him for just ten bidis?"

True, Haju couldn't do any of the jobs that the others in this world could. Maybe he was meant to do a different kind of work, a kind that he had never found.

Within a few days, someone else again brought him news of a job quite like that. A man called Imtiaz often visited the Hostel in the late hours of the night. He was a pleasant-looking, bearded and chubby fellow who worked as an assistant chef in a very large hotel. He came from the same village as Saifulla. Imtiaz was a rather entertaining man, he came here for a friendly chat with his friends. His visit usually created quite a stir, for he often brought with him rare delicacies like biriyani, chicken curry, and mince meat to name a few. But no one ever asked him whether he stole these from the hotel kitchen or whether they were leftovers and rejects.

Haju had never tasted such sumptuous food earlier. and he relished them. Imtiaz had also grown quite fond of Haju. Whenever he found others snubbing or misbehaving with him, he would immediately intervene. "Poor thing," He would say. "How many such innocent people could be found nowadays? Can't you see, someone who is not even aware of his own good can never do any harm to others!"

"Well, if a thief ever enters our house in the afternoon, I am sure our Haju will not move a finger." Saifulla sounded sarcastic. "He will just keep staring at him. In fact, he might even start being nice to them."

Imtiaz laughed aloud and said, "*Dulabhai*, the way things are now, can one really say who is a thief and who is not? Anyway, I think I can find Haju a job in my hotel."

"What?" The others exclaimed in surprise. Imtiaz was working in a big hotel, where so many *sahibs* and *memsahibs* stayed. A hotel where all the dignitaries from Delhi and Bombay put up. And it had such an amazingly spacious lobby, the like of which no one had ever seen! Once Kader had gone to meet Imtiaz for some personal help, but the hotel durwan had driven him off, saying that nobody could leave the kitchen during duty hours, and that no visitor could walk in either!

There was always a chance of earning a little extra in a hotel, for which many people had already placed a request for a possible job. But Imtiaz hadn't been able to help them. And today he was offering. Haju, of all people, a job?

Everybody was about to say something, but Saifulla, like a true leader, raised a hand and stopped them. Then he began to speak in a serious tone. "Listen Imtiaz," He said, "This is not a worthwhile proposition. It may eventually spell danger for you. Who knows what this ass might break, lose or spoil in the hotel. You never know ... he might even mix urine with water, and then even your own job might be at stake! One who couldn't even tie *bidis!* What work could he possibly do? Instead, let that good for nothing continue to keep living off others' mercy. After all, he's a creature of God and we can't get rid of him, can we?"

However, Imtiaz wasn't deterred by all this. He said, "There's nothing to fear, in the kind of job that he will be doing he will have nothing to break. In fact, it's a rather an easy one.

"Then why didn't you offer it to us?" Kader asked. "We have heard that there maybe a lock-out in our factory soon ..."

"Oh, you couldn't do that kind of work. Everybody is not fit for every kind of job! The job that I am referring to is one that only Haju can do. It would require someone to stand in one place the whole day, and keep saluting people from time to time."

Eklas said.

This time Nadeem and Kader spoke together. "But he'll definitely forget, he'll definitely forget to salute."

"Oh it wouldn't matter if he forgot once or twice. Nobody really notices it. It's alright if he can keep standing all day."

Eklas turned to Haju and asked – "Would you like to work in a hotel?"

Haju nodded his head instantly. He could already feel the aroma of all those delicious dishes ... those kababs, koftas, the biriyani ...!

Eklas himself took initiative and bought Haju a pair of trousers and shirts. After that, he took him to the hotel.

Within a few days, Haju grew immensely fond of his work. It was really such a wonderful job. There was no need to run around, no physical exertion, and no taking orders from a boss. It was so much easier than even making bidis.

All he had to do was to keep standing against a shining white wall of the gents' toilet in the Hotel India International. And whenever someone entered the toilet, he would have to salute him. When the gentlemen came to wash their hands, he had to offer them a soap and a towel, though not all of them used it.

Of course this was not a bathroom, it was only a toilet. Haju wondered whether even the all-knowing Saifulla knew that people could build such a beautiful room for something as trivial? The walls were so smoothly polished that they shone as bright as the sun. And the mirrors were so large! When he had nothing else to see, Haju kept looking at his own reflection in the mirror. His duty hours were from one o clock in the afternoon to eleven o clock at night, with only two breaks of half an hour each in between. For the rest of the time, he had to keep standing still. But Haju didn't mind that. After all these years in his life, he had at last found a shelter where nobody rebuked or beat him.

Of course the gentlemen who came to the toilet never spoke to him. Some of them didn't even notice him Again, there were others who tipped him some twenty or twenty five paise, just like that. There wasn't that much of a crowd in the day time, they generally started arriving after it was dark.

There were two bars on the ground floor. As the night progressed and the drunken revelry in those rooms increased, the gentlemen would start frequenting that immaculately white-painted room where Haju was on duty. It's not that he had not seen drunkards earlier. He knew that local liquor was often sold in their market at Gajipur. Even though he himself had never tasted it, he had seen a number of his acquaintances in an inebriated state. But the drunkards that he saw here were of a totally different kind. There were no drunken brawls or shouts. True, he had seen a few of them stagger, some of them spoke to the walls, and some even lost their balance. A few of them even seemed not to recognize their own reflections in the mirror.

Haju stood still against the wall, and kept watching them silently. He never offered help even if anyone was sick. Imtiaz had told him repeatedly that he should not talk to anyone unless spoken to and should not offer any help unless he was called. The strong smell of naphthalene that filled the room in the afternoon gradually changed to a stronger odour as the hours passed by!

One day two young men entered the room at about a quarter

to ten at night. Their eyes were reddish, their hair unkempt and they were staggering. Haju had by now got to know the faces of those who frequented the place. But he saw these men for the first time. And whenever he saw someone for the first time, he would observe him more intently, and try to hear what the man said more carefully, even though he couldn't understand most of what these two said to each other.

The two young men were apparently poets. It wasn't usual for poets to visit such luxury hotels, but sometimes some well-to do admirer would bring them here.

One of the poets looked at the wall and said, "I just cant stand this. It irritates me every time I see him."

The other poet too stared at the wall and asked, "Which one? It's that short fellow with that girl, isn't it? Oh, he's talking too much and boring us to death! I think I am going to hit him now."

The first poet said, "No, its not that. It's that attendant there. Tell me, does it make any sense to have an attendant inside an urinal?"

"Well, its only a British legacy, just a vulgar aping of a western style."

"But are such practices followed in England now?"

"It was only in the colonies that they imposed such vulgar practices."

"And now this nation has become a Marwari colony!"

The two men walked upto the basin to wash their hands. One of them started sprinkling water on his face and eyes, while the other gazed into his own reflection in the mirror. Haju stood still, holding a soap and towel.

One of the poets suddenly turned around and looked Haju straight in the eye. "Where do you live? Where are you from?" He asked, his voice almost a drunken shriek.

Haju stared back silently, like a cow tied to a pole. He couldn't find an answer to this sudden question.

Drunkards have a certain stubbornness in them. It seemed as if this man wouldn't be able to swallow the next peg if he didn't get an answer from Haju right away. He put a finger on Haju's chin, and tilted his face. "Why don't you answer?" He demanded, looking into his eyes. "Where do you live?"

Haju shook a little and said, "Gajipur, Sahib."

"Which district?"

"Midnapore."

"What is your name?"

"Haju."

"Haju? Can anybody have such a name? Did I ask what name your parents call you by? I want to know what your proper name is!"

Well that was the name that people called him by, ever since he was born. Though, he did have another name, it hadn't been used for a very long time.

"Shajan, Sahib!" Haju uttered rather quickly.

"What a peculiar man!" The poet said in an irritated manner. "What a peculiar name! Have you ever heard of anyone called 'Shajan'? Are you a Hindu or a Muslim?"

In a tearful voice that could hardly be heard, Haju said, "We are Muslims."

The second man burst into laughter. and said, "Don't you see! It's Shahjehan! So tell me dear Shahjehan, how did you get confined in this toilet? What happened to the Agra Fort?"

The first poet patted his friend's shoulder and said, "Come on, lets'go! This is simply disgusting! We are still complying with such systems, we are still not being able to kick the manager out ..."

"Oh, you think of such noble things only after gulping down five pegs, I am sure these thoughts will vanish by tomorrow morning. How will it help to kick the manager, anyway? Instead, he will only stop us from entering this place ever again!"

"Still, I will surely kick him some day!"

The second poet staggered upto the door. Then he suddenly turned towards Haju and said, "*Salaam Samrat*! At one time, you ruled over the entire Hindustan, and now you remain locked up in this toilet! Well ... Good night!"

The words of the two gentlemen didn't leave a mark on Haju. He had hardly understood anything! Of course, these were all whims of drunken men! It was enough that they didn't beat him or break his head!

But even before its aftermath had died, another Bengali man entered the toilet. He moved to a cubicle in the corner, then while unzipping himself, asked Haju, "Is it true that you are called Shahjehan? Ha, ha, ha, ha!!"

Apparently, the two poets who had come here earlier had made great fun of this name in the bar. Finally, they had become so inebriated that they had to be thrown out. But since then, many people came to know that the insignificant man waiting in the toilet was called Shahjehan. After that, people often called him by that name. "Hey you Shahjehan, give me a towel, will you!" They said, laughing among themselves.

Of course this sudden increase in the status of his name didn't affect Haju in any way. Many a times he couldn't even understand that they were addressing him, when called by that name. The *babus* pronounced it so differently, besides it was difficult to follow what they said a drunken manner.

It was actually the afternoon hours that Haju liked most. Other than Saturdays and Sundays, there was hardly a visitor between three and six in the afternoon. Then he could, if he wished to, even go out for a while. But he never did. He just stood still and gazed at the bright shining walls. To him, there was nothing more beautiful than that!

One afternoon, he suddenly noticed a row of ants crawling down the wall. It was a long row of red ants moving in a very disciplined manner, with none of them breaking out of the line. Haju wasn't interested to know why those ants were crawling down that bathroom wall, or where they were going to. How beautiful it looked – that row of red ants on the shining white wall! Haju stared in enchantment! Suddenly he remembered the procession that he had seen near Sulemanpur, on his way here! That long line of people from the side of the canal making their way across the bridge! Hadn't that procession also looked something like this?

Haju took some water from the tap and drew a line on the wall. "This was the canal, and this here ... was the bridge." He said to himself. The wall was so slippery that the water just wouldn't stand. So Haju started broadening the lines with more water. The row of ants came and stopped near that line. A few of them moved from the front on to the two sides of the line and stood still. A few others started running back, as if they were about to discuss something

Haju was taken aback! Wouldn't the row of ants cross over the bridge to the other side of the canal? How interesting indeed! He lowered his tone to almost a whisper and said – "That's good dears, why go that side? Why fight unnecessarily? After all, there is a lot of space on this side too."

As soon as he broadened the line with a little more water, the row of ants turned around and started moving in a different direction. Haju stared in amazement! It was as if he had never felt happier. These ants had heeded his words! Yes, they had obeyed him!

Overwhelmed, Haju began to draw lines at random. "Here, this side, this side ..."

He kept whispering, as his hand moved against the wall, in silent ecstacy.

Damayanti's Face
Damayantir Mukh

It was a bright and sunny morning with no trace of mist or cloud. The mountain peaks in the distance dazzled in the sunlight, making it difficult for one to glance in that direction. A light breeze blew, not smoothly, but rather erratically as if it was playing a game of its own. Suddenly, a woodpecker flew in from somewhere and perched close to Archishman. There weren't any tall trees around, and yet the bird often flew in from God knows where. It was a beautiful, majestic looking bird. With a head shaped like a crown and a body covered with silken feathers, it moved around with slow, arrogant steps. Archishman stared at the bird in silent rapture. In fact every time he saw it, he felt a sense of endless amazement.

Having just come out of the cave, Archishman felt happy to see this beautiful morning. He wasn't feeling too well, in fact he hadn't slept well last night. It was some kind of an uneasiness that had kept him awake, and he had to sit up often to rub his troubled chest. Of course, there was no question of taking any medicines, he hadn't taken any for the last forty years or so. Sitting in that vast nocturnal silence amidst the surrounding mountains, he had tried to quieten his own heart. 'Calm down calm down' he had whispered. 'leave me if you must, but go peacefully.'

His chest still felt heavy this morning and his limbs felt weak. But his mind soon surpassed his ailing body and drowned in the magnificence of the scenic beauty all around. He sat gazing at the woodpecker's dancing feet for a few more moments. Then wrapping a blanket around himself, he went and sat on the boulder that he had once named "*Garud's* throne." In fact he had named every stone that lay around this cave. There were two others that were named "*Mahakurma*" and "*Thir Bijuri*." Somehow, for some strange reason, the last one had seemed like a woman to him, so he never used it as a seat.

After the woodpecker, it was the butterflies' turn. It was only on such bright sunny mornings that these beautiful creatures were seen, no one knew where they hid during rain and fog! After fluttering around for a while, the butterflies came and sat on the tiny grass-flowers. What beautifully coloured wings they had! Even after so many years, these little creatures continued to amaze Archishman! He was yet to figure out the secret of their beauty! How easily they sat on the tiniest of flowers and swayed in the breeze, as if they were completely weightless!

It was now time for a wash. The river wasn't too far, in fact with no other sounds nearby, the gurgling sound of the waters could be heard from the entrance to the cave itself. But somehow

Archishman was feeling rather lazy to walk even that short distance this morning. When he finally stood up after a while, he felt a severe pain searing through his waist, the like of something he had never experienced earlier. Could it be his advancing age? Maybe he was really getting old! He quickly turned his attention from himself to the butterflies nearby. "Beautiful, beautiful" he whispered again, in quiet admiration.

The path sloped downward to the river, and was therefore quite easy to descend, but to prevent himself from stumbling, Archishman continued to move by holding on to the boulders on one side. It filled him with great joy to see the river for the first time every morning. There was nothing in this world that he possessed as his own, and yet, each time he saw the river he felt as if it belonged to him.

Actually, it was only a very tiny river that started from the snow capped mountains, and then mingled with another river nearby. It had no name of its own, and Archishman had named it *Kharsha*. Somehow, that name had now spread among the local people here and so it would continue to remain even after he was long gone!

The water was freezing! So many years had passed by, but still Archishman had to wait a while before he could dip his hand in the waters! As a child, he had always felt reluctant to bathe in the cold winter months. He remembered how he would first throw the towel into the pond and wait for it to all but sink before taking the plunge himself. It was still the same way now. But he didn't have a towel here, he let the water dry on the skin itself.

He sat by the riverside and then bent down and looked at his own reflection in the waters. There was very little that could be seen on that heavily bearded face; it was as if he was seeing himself after a long, long time, and it seemed rather unfamiliar. The brightness in his eyes had dimmed – a possible indication of his illness. But not wanting to be deterred by his own physical ailment, he looked up at the sky. Surely, such a clear blue could not be seen anywhere else in the world. It was very uncommon here too, and nobody could tell when and how soon this blue would give way to dark clouds and a raging storm. In fact, even on the last full moon day, a violent storm had ravaged the mountains for three days, without stopping even for a moment.

Looking at that azure blue now, Archishman forgot his own physical pain. He was amazed to see how untouched the sky remained through the ages. The passage of time had failed to leave even a mark on it, and it was indeed, ever-young.

Suddenly he heard someone greet him from the other side of the river. The words "Namaste Bangali Baba" – echoed across the waters, and Archishman turned to see a middle-aged man rushing by with a young lamb in his arms. The lamb seemed injured, and the man was possibly carrying it to Shirshi Baba's ashram. After all, Shirshi Baba's touch could bring back to health, not only ailing people but also birds and animals.

Archishman raised his hand and blessed him. "May you live long." he said, but the man didn't have the time to speak any more. He seemed to be in great hurry.

Even though so many years had passed by, people here still addressed Archishman as 'Bangali Baba'. His own Guru Jogatrayananda had once given him a different name. After draping the saffron robe over him, he had named him

"*Basabheswarswami*", but somehow that name hadn't stuck. Over the years, Archishman had learnt Hindi quite well, as it was by and large, the *lingua franca* of the sadhus in the hills, but his Bengali accent hadn't left him. Somehow one could easily make out that he was a Bengali after hearing him speak just two or three sentences of Hindi.

Interestingly, Archishman's name from his worldly life hadn't yet vanished, and it was really surprising that some people still remembered it. It was only last December, when two young men from the city had come in search of him. They had wanted to publish his interview in their own little magazine. Archishman had of course found the idea extremely amusing. Why, he had wondered, would anybody be interested in interviewing a sadhu who had distanced himself from human habitation for so many years?

In any case, he didn't really have any message for others, he was still searching for some enlightenment himself. But, he had felt kindly towards these young boys who had braved the long climb just to meet him. Even though he didn't answer any of their enthusiastic questions, he had patted them affectionately on their back. He didn't even wish to read the magazines that the boys had left behind, in fact he couldn't remember the last time he had read a printed word. There was no need to keep any count of time here, and it was only because the year 1995 was printed on those magazines, that he suddenly realised that as many as thirty six years had passed by since he had first sought shelter in these mountains.

Those boys had also informed him that the National Library in Calcutta still preserved the index cards in his name, and that one could still find his book of poetry there. In fact, a renowned litterateur had apparently dedicated two full pages of his recently published autobiography to Archishman Guha Thakurta. It was from the book that those boys had got to know about him. But even after he heard all that, Archishman hadn't felt any special curiosity to enquire about anything, he had only smiled in response. In answer to their repeated queries as to why he had denounced worldly life and taken refuge in these mountains, he had said that it was only his own 'destiny' that had brought him there.

But did man really guide his own destiny? Or is it that deep inside the human mind, there are certain processes that defy all logic?

It was in the year 1959, that a team of eleven mountaineers from Chandennagore had set out on an expedition to the Sundardunga glaciers. The team was led by a young poet who had no earlier experiences of trekking. In fact he had almost forced the organizers to include him in that team. Had he then experienced, as people say, a 'call of the mountains'? No, it hadn't been quite that. The base camp had been set up in Umla but by then the young leader was already fraught with exhaustion and cold, and worse still, nursing a knee-injury. He just couldn't go on any further. After completing their expedition successfully, the rest of the team returned and spent one more night at Umla, to celebrate their victory. But, the next day, as they were preparing to go back, the young man had suddenly announced that he would like to stay back in the mountains, for a few more days. His friends tried to reason with him to give up his whim, but the young man remained firm. Of course, initially he had planned to spend only a month in the beautiful surroundings enshrined by those majestic mountains, but as time passed, and months gave way to years, and the years to decades, he suddenly realised that all of three decades had passed by.

It was true that he had not planned it this way when he had started out from Calcutta, nor had he felt any deep spiritual urge earlier. Instead, he had always enjoyed the company of his fellow poets and the usual thrills of a urban life. So, how did the aesthetic beauty of nature suddenly begin to attract him? Was it then a secret hurt that he was fighting against – a memory of some woman perhaps? There was of course a reason of that sort, but it was only secondary.

It was almost thirty six years back, at around the time of the expedition, that Damayanti and her husband had come and rented a flat in his neighbourhood. In fact the two houses were so close that the windows almost opened out to each other. Every morning, Archishman would see Damayanti and her husband sitting in their balcony and sipping tea – a sight that he found just unbearable.

Was it then for that alone, that he never returned from the mountains? But that would have been very childish indeed. For after all, he could have easily moved over to Krishnanagar where he was teaching at the time, and also enjoyed the very favourable literary ambience of the place. So, he didn't really have to take refuge in these distant mountains just to stay away from her! Was it then his destiny, or only a whim that made him stay back, at least initially? It wasn't that he felt a strong secret hurt or anger towards anybody, rather his own poetic persona had flourished in the ethereal ambience among the mountains. But such feelings do not last long, so it would have been natural for him to return to the city after a while!

There was of course one man here who had attracted him and that was Sadhu Yogatrayananda who lived some distance away. Archishman was curious to know what it was about the sadhu that attracted the local people there. So one day, he set out for the ashram himself. Archishman's own views on religion were quite liberal. Though he himself didn't practice any particular religion, he was not disrespectful towards others' faiths. After all, people had the right to their own beliefs. His own ideas about the existence of a Supreme God was rather vague. It was really difficult to say whether there was indeed such a Supreme being who created and guided the entire universe! At times he felt that God existed only in peoples' imagination while on other occasions, he wondered if God was really responsible for creating this beautiful world and ensuring the continued benevolence of all creatures, why couldn't He see the ugliness, enmity, and the growing evil rampant among the people?

Before stepping into the ashram, Archishman spent some time in the beautifully maintained garden outside, roaming around the flowers. He was enchanted by the riot of different colours, designs and shapes and most of all by the sheer underlying perfection of all that he saw! Who had created this variety, he wondered! Had not a thoughtful mind worked behind this creation? How else could there have been so many different types of plants! It wasn't only the flowers, there were so many different species, so many kinds of plants, human beings, animals, birds and insects as well! Things that were made in a factory were only prototypes of each other. Could it then be that in nature's own workshop, there existed an artist named God? On the other hand, it was difficult to imagine a single artist sitting somewhere and drawing so many millions of designs in each category?

Archishman walked into the ashram, and found Yogibaba sitting on a tiger skin laid out in an open courtyard. He was a tall and well built man with no harsh lines on his face. It felt rather nice to look at him. At the time, he was talking to some of his disciples in a hushed voice without any tone of imposition. On that very first day, Archishman had not spoken a word; he had just sat and observed the Baba for a while, and then left the place.

It was true that earlier, Archishman used to consider this act of sanctimony as some kind of a commercial activity that didn't need any initial capital or hard work to prosper. All it required was an ability to speak a few impressive words, and those words attracted and retained the allegiance of a few disciples who in turn looked after the guru's well being. It seemed strange that even though quoting examples was not the same as stating logic, somehow all sadhus seemed to charm their disciples by frequently quoting similies in their discourses! Not only that, in reply to peoples' serious questions, they usually narrated only simple stories!

The peaceful environment of the ashram nestling in the backdrop of the serene mountains with its beautiful garden in front had appealed to Archishman. The Yogibaba himself often roamed around the garden, caressing each of the radiant flowers.

One day, after he had visited the ashram for about three times, Archishman asked Yogibaba why he had built the ashram there and whether he had really gained anything spiritually. In reply,

Yogibaba had stood amidst the flowers and pointed to the sky. "That is what I have got." He had said, rather mysteriously.

Archishman was taken aback at this response. Was it then, such an easy answer after all? Even the greatest of saints and meditators never directly admitted their realisation of God. They usually meandered to other topics. Was this man then a fake, a liar?

"You mean you have already seen God?"

Had Yogibaba answered 'yes' to this, Archishman would have certainly never come here a second time. But Baba had only smiled a little and said – "No, I do not know whether God really lives up there or not. I have not seen Him yet, I had pointed at the sky to imply that I have been able to realise and feel the sky. When I look at trees, I feel them, when I look at people, I also feel them, but the sky is above everything!"

The words and the soft tone of his voice had impressed Archisman. He had felt as if he was hearing a poet speak!

After Archishman had got to know him well, Yogibaba invited him to come and live in his ashram. Till then, Archishman had been living in a villager's house. He had to pay them just two rupees a day, and in return they would cook and serve him his meals. He didn't even have to pay any rent for his lodging. So, it was partly Yogibaba's personality that had attracted Archishman to give up such conveniences and move to the ashram. Of course he didn't have to follow any set pattern of rules here. Yogibaba had not even asked him to conform to any spiritual rituals or meditations, in fact he had said that Archishman could do whatever he wanted to. "Just look around and see the mountains, the rivers, the trees, see them carefully, look right into the core of their beings, that itself will purify your heart." He had said.

There were times when Archishman, out of a restlessness in keeping with youth, had tried to outwit Yogibaba by asking him several questions, but he had never succeeded. One day he asked, "You say that God is all benevolent. Then why can't he see the evil and animosity prevailing around the world? Do you know that an atom bomb had been used to destroy millions of lives in Japan? Were all those innocent people sinners? Why did they die and why did those killers go unpunished? Tell me, what kind of a game was the Almighty playing?"

Yogibaba had given a very simple answer.

"I really have no answer to that." He had said. "Nobody has given me the duty to speak on His behalf either. I keep seeking God only for my own mental peace. I do not know whether I will ever get to see Him. But at times I do feel an indication of His presence and I live with the hope that one day I shall at least feel the radiance of His divine halo."

On another day, Archishman had asked, "Why must one have to seek Him? Let Him be, if He exists. I know some people who don't believe in the existence of God, and who don't feel concerned about Him either. They never cheat others, never lie unnecessarily and they live honest, clean lives."

"Good, very good." Yogibaba had remarked. "Of course, people have their own likes and dislikes. But I have seen how disturbing a lack of faith can be, and how peaceful a life, otherwise. If people can live peacefully even without having any faith, then let them do so. They are also to be respected."

After a moment's pause, he had continued, "There are also

some who move from disbelief to belief in this life itself, even though the path in-between is very long and arduous. But once they reach the ultimate destination, they find peace, such endless peace!. One cannot experience that kind of tranquillity without attaining that goal. Somehow, I feel that you may be able to achieve it, you will reach that goal some day, I know."

Archishman had taken those words rather lightly. "Alright, let's see." He had said casually.

About a month and a half later, Archishman's father had come to take him back. Archishman had lost his mother at a very young age. Since then he had grown up in a family that had consisted of his father, two brothers, a sister and an aunt. But, Archishman did not want to return. His father's coaxing and tearful requests failed to move him.

"I'll return when I feel like." He had said. "But for now, I just want to remain and see for myself how much longer I like it here. Till then, I'll keep writing to you."

After that, his elder brother and a couple of friends had made another attempt to dissuade him from his staying on in the mountain. But Archishman was still in such a state of infatuation with his surroundings, that it was not possible to force or cajole him back to the city.

Yogibaba had told him that one couldn't realise God just by closing one's eyes and meditating frantically for hours. After all, His divine touch lay within every creature on of this earth. That is why it was necessary to get to know the trees, flowers, birds, rivers and mountains first. It was within those that His radiance would first be noticed.

Since then, Archishman had tried to look around and acquaint himself with nature. Sometimes, he would sit from morning to evening, in front of a flowering tree ,watching the buds bloom. He would see the bees and butterflies play, and see in it – the flow of life. One could make out why flowers bloomed so beautifully. Of course the bees didn't have to dress so well! But why did the butterflies come so beautifully dressed? Why were their wings so exquisitely designed? Every creation of nature had some purpose to serve, but where was the need for such eloborate design on the wings of these butterflies when they had such short lives and, when they served only as food for birds!

Archishman's meditation involved sitting quietly by the side of the flowering tree, on the bank of the Kirana river. However, he would often get distracted by thoughts of Damayanti. Though there were scars in his heart, he no longer felt any overwhelming sadness for her. In fact he had started to withdraw from her long before she had got married.

It was during a merry go round ride at a fair ground in Shantiniketan, that the two had first met. Both were accompanied by their friends that day. It was an attraction right from the start! After being introduced to each other, they had spent the next few hours together, eating from food stalls and exchanging addresses. Damayanti had come from Asansol, and Archishman lived somewhere near the Dum Dum cantonment.

It was not Archishman who had written the first letter. After reading one of his poems, Damayanti had sent him a letter full of praise. This started a flood of letters between the two. It started with one or two letters a week, followed by a letter a day. Sometimes, Archishman even wrote her two letters on the same day.

Like a teething child always anxious to bite, a young poet too felt the urge to take up a pen and write. It was almost as if he had lived his entire life through his writing, breathed through his writing and found in it a liberating process. It wasn't only poetry that Archishman composed then, he also wrote book reviews, essays, and travelogues. The editor of the *Desh* had once praised his prose-style and asked whether he would like to write a novel for his magazine. In reply, Archishman had bowed his head in modesty, though he had felt overjoyed at this unexpected but very coveted proposal!

After that, Archishman and Damayanti went on writing to each other constantly for three years. In this period, he met her only once. Damayanti had come to attend her cousin's wedding in Calcutta, and the two had met, as per plan, near the waterfront on the grounds of the Victoria Memorial. They had walked side by side, they couldn't talk freely to each other as they had done in their letters. They didn't even touch each other, at least not quite. Only once, Archishman touched one of her delicate champak-like fingers, and that at the time, had seemed rewarding enough.

By then, Archishman's first book of poems had got published by a small publishing house. After receiving a copy of the book, Damayanti had written to him, "You must send me a copy of every poem before you publish it. I want to be the first to read it. After all, you are my own poet and I am confident that my poet will win the Nobel prize one day."

After three years, Damayanti had come to Calcutta for her postgraduate studies. She had made arrangements to stay with her uncle's family in Tollygunj, but it was very far from

Archishman 's own place in Dum Dum. It was a large house with many persons living in it; there were no restrictions on boys and girls mixing freely with each other. Archishman had often visited her there. There were two living rooms on the ground floor, and it wasn't difficult to talk in private in the afternoon hours.

Archishman remembered that day very clearly. It was a cloudy afternoon, and they had spent many hours together in the smaller living room. An old fashioned sofa was placed next to a wall. On the other side of the room stood a marble table with four chairs round it. Damayanti had sat on the sofa dressed in a smoky grey saree and her hair hung loose. Archishman sat on a chair, at a little distance, with a cigarette in hand. Dressed casually in a shirt and trousers, he looked as if he hadn't shaved or combed his hair for a while. Outside the open window, a *karabi* tree swayed in the late afternoon breeze. Clouds were thundering in the sky and a heavy shower seemed imminent. From time to time, the two of them stopped talking and looked at each other. After all, there were times when silence could convey so much more than words! Their hearts flowed to each other through their eyes. But for the first time, it wasn't only their hearts which rejoiced, they felt it in their veins too. It was clear that they attracted each other like magnets, in fact Archishman could leave his chair any moment and walk up to her.

But that much coveted moment did not arrive. The next instant, footsteps were heard on the wooden staircase nearby and two young men entered the room. It was Damayanti's elder brother Tapan and his friend Abhijit, an officer in the Air Force.

Abhijit was a tall, and very handsome young man, well dressed, with neatly combed hair.

Since that day Abhijit was often seen in that house , and the three would spend a lot of time together in friendly talk. It was obvious that Abhijit didn't much care for Bengali poetry, but he wasn't badly read either. He was well acquainted with foreign literature and was somewhat fluent in German language as well.

A few days later, a troupe of foreign dancers came to perform at the ice-skating rink in the city, and Abhijit suggested that they all go and see it. Apparently, he knew someone, who could get them tickets easily. Damayanti was of course very eager, and agreed to the proposal instantly. Tapan said that he couldn't go because he had to see a lawyer for some personal reason. Archishman on his part, looked deep into Damayanti's eyes and said, "I can't go either, I have some other work." Damayanti tried to coax him. But Archishman didn't agree. He wanted to see if Damayanti would still go with Abhijit. Finally, only the two of them went.

That was the day that their relationship ended. Of course, Abhijit had taken her out earlier also, but that day Tapan had accompanied them. It had been to a dinner at the Great Eastern Hotel – a treat that Archisman could never afford!

But did it really matter if Damayanti accompanied Abhijit to the dance performance? No, it didn't, Archishman knew that. But he realised that a silent war had started. Of course he was not going to take part in this battle. After all Abhijit was an armed warrior. And what was he? Nothing but a poet. Could there possibly be a fight between the two? Poets never liked to engage in any kind of competition. It was not that they were afraid to do so, it was just a matter of distaste for them. Of course people would think this to be a defeat for him. Let them think like that. Such self-acclaimed defeat only resulted in inflating a poet's ego, which in turn boosted his creativity!

After that, Archishman never visited Tollygunge again. Fifteen days later, he received a letter from Damayanti. She wrote again when he did not answer. But what could Archishman say to her? Hadn't she understood that he had tried to stop her from going out with Abhijit that evening? If she had failed to read the message in his eyes that day, what was the point of writing letters?

Six months later, Abhijit and Damayanti were married. Ever since he had secured a good job, Abhijit had been on the look out for a suitable bride. Once he selected Damayanti, marriage was inevitable. After all, he had come only to win!

It was true that the news hadn't hurt Archishman too much. He had blamed only himself, it was as if he had destroyed the idol he had once sculpted with his own hands!

But why did Abhijit have to rent a house near the Dum Dum cantonment? Maybe he did not know where Archishman lived. But Damayanti knew! Now, they would often meet on the roads. They would have to interact and visit each other as neighbours, maybe Abhijit would invite him over for a cup of tea, and some day he would even have to witness Damayanti step into motherhood! All these thoughts had ravaged his heart.

But that was not why he had escaped to the mountains. Maybe there had always been a hidden love for nature in his heart. The majestic silence of the Himalayas had truly impressed him! After all, what really mattered in life. was this feeling of tranquillity.

There were some in this world who liked mastery over others, and others who preferred solitude.

After coming in contact with Yogibaba, Archishman's own outlook had broadened quite substantially. He realised that one could love even a tree as passionately. A bunch of flowers or even a meandering river could be the objects of one's affection. At times, he even experienced an extra sensory perception. It was as if there was some kind of an energy behind everything that was visible. Even the changing colours of an evening sky made him wonder whether that was not really the manifestation of God's mercy!

Of course he couldn't forget Damayanti completely. That was not possible. At times, her face loomed large before his eyes, blotting out even the enormous mountains in the background. But the next minute, that face disintegrated into pieces.

Archishman hadn't known any other woman intimately before he met Damayanti, and he did not get to know anyone afterward either. There had been a moment when he had almost come close to holding her in ardent embrace, but that did not materialize. Intimacy with a woman was something that remained hidden from him for ever. But he had no regrets for that. Nature was no less enchanting than a woman. If one could experience the true glory of God, then the mind would never turn to anything else.

One day, something happened that left Archishman feeling terribly perturbed. The memory of that cloudy afternoon in Damayanti's house, and the intense looks that they had exchanged suddenly flashed in his mind and he felt his own passion begin to rise. His blood began to rush, and he felt a certain restlessness in his body.

What was happening to him, he wondered? He did not desire Damayanti any more, then why this restlessness? Wasn't the body under the control of the mind? A shadow of guilt fell over him. After sitting still for a long time, Archishman went to see Yogibaba.

The two of them often had frank discussion on various matters. So, Archishman related the incident to him without any hesitation. After listening to it all, Yogibaba closed his eyes and sat silently as if in deep meditation.

After a while, he said "See, how warm my body has grown. Feel it." He took one of Archishman's hands in his own and placed it on his groin.

Then, seeing Archishman' dazed face, he said, "Son, I have never experienced any physical intimacy. Nor have I left behind a beloved, like you. Ever since I was a child, I have had a passionate urge to unite with God, Such physical arousals can manifest from a strong desire to unite with someone. That is how the body acts. You don't have to think of a woman to be aroused."

Yogibaba's words had finally come true. Damayanti had slowly faded away from his mind and there came a day when he couldn't even remember her face. But of course that had been much later.

After Yogibaba had passed away, Archishman left that ashram, and took refuge in a cave higher up in the mountains. Jogibaba had always desired that Archishman take over the responsibility of his ashram, but seeing it become the cause of rift among the other disciples, Archishman had withdrawn. After all, not all sadhus were of the same mettle. He had seen many who were quite selfish.

There was no need to worry for food in his new abode. Archishman never cooked anything for himself. There was a community mess in a village called Potala, about five miles from here, run by a Gujarati committee. He didn't have to go there either, there were some volunteers who brought him his daily quota of bread, *chatu, gud* and *batasha*. It was only on days of heavy rain or storm that they couldn't come. Not that it really mattered, because the human body could remain healthy even without eating for a day or two. It was only the mind that constantly worried about whether the boys would finally bring the food or not.

Two days before he died, Yogibaba lost his power of speech. Archishman had always nourished a great desire to know whether he had finally seen the light of God or not. He noticed a beatific smile on the Baba's face the last day. What had he finally received?

The fact that there was something hidden in the world whose 'magnificence' would be found some day is what lends excitement to life. Whether it was the changing shadows over the mountain throughout the day, or the sound of thunder in the sky, there seemed to be a mystery in everything around. Not a single day that Archishman spent in the hills had seemed repetitive or boring. He didn't need to read the scriptures, he had already chanced on a realisation from within the variety in the universe.

After a bath in the river, Archishman came and stood in the sun, his body still wet. He felt a hammering in his heart. Why was everything so troubling today? He looked around for the woodpecker, but couldn't find it. It had flown away. Even the butterflies weren't there. He looked up at the sky, and whispered – "Oh you beauteous one, make me forget my body now."

Somehow, it seemed cooler today. Compared to cloudy days, it was always cooler when the sun shone brightly. After so many years here, his body had got accustomed to the severest cold and he could do with just one blanket.

Wrapping the blanket a little tighter around his drenched body, Archishman walked slowly towards the cave. He wished he could lie down for a while, it would be nice if he could light a fire and rest in its warmth. But that was not to be, he couldn't even reach up to the caves. He suddenly stumbled, and his forehead hit a hard rock. He tried hard to raise himself but his whole body felt paralysed. Was this then the last moment in his life? If it was, then so be it. He had no complaint.

Suddenly, it felt as if the pain that he had been experiencing till this moment had disappeared. It was as if the body itself was gone, it was only the mind now, and that too felt completely weightless. A look of admiration slowly crept into his face as scenes, one after another passed by his eyes. A pile of molten gold flowed down from the mountain tops, then the gold changed into a very soothing, white coloured smoke. Somewhere in the distance the bells rang in chorus for the evening Arati. A number of butterflies resembling a flower petal flew in and covered the stone in front of where he lay. And then, a sudden ray of light piereced through the smoke.

Was that the halo of God? Glory, glory to this life. There was nothing so supremely beautiful as this light. And then, a face appeared from within that ray of light. It was Damayanti's. At first Archishman was not able to recognize it, he felt amazed.

Was this God's own form? No, of course not, it was Damayanti, the Damayanti from his young days, the one whose hand he had touched only once. But he had not remembered her at all in the years towards the end, And yet, it was exactly that face that he saw now, a face covered in grief.

"Archi, you hadn't ever loved me." Damayanti said a in a voice full of weariness.

"Why talk about that that now?" Archishman said. "Why did you come here? I am not the Archishman that you once knew. Why did you suddenly come and hide the Lord's halo from me?"

Damayanti didn't seem to hear him. "You didn't love me." She said again. "You had only loved a woman whom you had created yourself. All the letters that you had written to me, were actually meant for your own self. You had not wanted me, and that is why you had given me up to another man at the very first opportunity, and moved far away."

"No, that's not true." There was a pleading earnestness in Archishman's voice now. "Till the time that no one else came between us, I had loved you. And there was no insincerity in that."

"Is this what you call love?" Damayanti said. "I had called you through my letters, but you hadn't replied. And then you left me and moved far away. You didn't think of me even once in all these years."

"Damayanti, I have not loved any other woman in my life. I had not interacted with any other woman lest I forget you. And, I have preserved that love intact in my heart. I cannot tell you how it hurt me initially every time I remembered you. It was because of that, that I had gradually transformed the memory of your face in my mind. I had split and merged that image with everything around me – those mountains, this small river, the blooming flowers, the butterflies and even that woodpecker. You are in everything that I see – the changing colours in the sky, the fragrance in the breeze, and even the shape of that stone. Come close Damayanti ... help me up."

And then, that ray of light merged with Archishman's lifeless body.

A Cup of Tea at the Taj Mahal
Taj Mahale ek Cup Cha

"*Ram Ram Ustadji*! What's the good news!"

Ustadji, whom the villagers greeted, sat draped in a heavily patched cloak-like robe. A piece of cloth was tied around his head and his chin had a week-long rough stubble. He was about fifty years old. Nobody knew where he lived, whether he had a wife or a son of his own. Each time he was asked about his family, he would only smile mysteriously.

Ustadji visited the village from time to time and exchanged tales of joy and sorrow with the villagers, sometimes advising them in time of trouble and need. He would spend a day or two with a family here and there, eating *chatu, roti*,vegetables or whatever they offered him, and would disappear again.

People still remembered how at the time of the drought last year, Ustadji had helped them deal with the village contractor who had behaved in such a shameless and cruel way. Had it been proper on the contractor's part to have stalled the on-going construction work of the bridge? In the absence of a seasonal crop, and with no money in hand, how could people have survived without a government salary? It was then that Ustadji had intervened. The villagers had got together and confined the contractor under a date palm, without food for a full twenty four hours!

During the days that Ustadji visited the village, there would always be a lot of fun. Of course one had to work hard throughout the day, the villagers knew that they were destined to toil till the last day of their lives. Those daily struggles and hard work erased all thoughts of joy and fun from their minds. It was precisely those happy thoughts that the Ustadji aroused in them. He would pat them on their back and say, "Of course you have to work hard, but that doesn't mean that you shouldn't feel happy! Can't you see, even the animals in the forests and the birds flying in the sky live so happily!"

Every evening, Ustadji would sit down with the others and engage in various discussions. Sometimes he would even start singing himself. Not that he had a particularly musical voice but it had a certain forcefulness and whenever he sang, he would place one hand on his ear, and stretch out the other in front of him, in the true style of an *Ustad*. It was because of this style that people referred him as Ustadji.

Ustadji generally carried a newspaper in his pocket. He was a literate man, and aware of the larger country and the world that lay beyond this village. In fact, one day he had pointed to the sky and told the villagers that even in that space that lay much above the ground and was far beyond man's sight, people were preparing to fight. Who knew, whether Ustadji made up such stories just for fun!

Hearing his voice now, a few others came and joined him. They squatted on the ground around the old man Ramkhelaon's cot, and then after greeting him by turn, said, "Tell us Ustadji, what is the good news in the papers today?"

"None really," Ustadji said "Do these newspapers ever carry stories about poor men like us? They only talk about rich businessmen and ministers. How would that interest you?"

Old Ramkhelaon smiled a toothless smile and said – "*Arre Ustadji*, what is there to write about a poor man's life? We too don't want to hear anything about the poor. Why don't you tell us stories about businessmen and ministers instead."

A young woman, Phoolsaria, joined in. " Last time you had told us a very amusing story about some village called Africa, why don't you tell us another story like that now!"

Phoolsaria's husband Dhania also had a query, "Ustadji, isn't it true that Indiraji's son Rajivji has now come to power? Do you know how many sons he has and how old they are? May the Lord never will it, but suppose Rajivji ever dies ..."

Immediately, some started laughing while others looked on in great concern. This wasn't a laughing matter at all, and they wanted to hear Ustadji's opinion on this.

There was no work to be done today. The sky looked very dry, and that is why they hadn't started work in the fields yet. It was only an eager, anxious waiting for the rains now. Time seemed to pass by ever so slowly!

Suddenly, Ustadji paused, and said, "Can any of get me a cup of tea?"

People stared at each other in silent embarrassment. It wasn't it shameful that even though this man had asked for just a simple cup of tea, they wouldn't be able to offer him that? How could they? After all, nobody here was used to you drinking tea.

Ustadji loked at their anxious faces, and realised what was wrong. Wasn't it only from his own frequent visits to the city that he had developed an addiction for tea?

He immediately raised a hand and said, "Doesn't matter, I don't need tea. Just get me a glass of water, one of you. After that I'll tell you the story of some businessman."

One young man immediately stood up and addressed the others. "There's a tea stall near the *pakki*. I can go and get some tea from that Sardar's hotel, if one of you just get me something to fetch it in."

The word *pakki* meant a proper road, or a highway. It was about two and a half miles from here, and the young man would have to run all the way and back!

Dhania found the idea very unpractical. " But if you run that far to fetch the tea, then you yourself might return feeling warm, but the tea will get cold, and there could be nothing more tasteless than that, worse than a cat's urine ..." He grimaced as if he was actually drinking the same, sending the people into fits of laughter.

"But couldn't we warm the tea again?" Phoolsaria suggested, silencing the others. Then she looked at the young man and said- "Go and fetch the tea quickly."

"And carry a big container so that you can bring lots of it." Ramkhelaon added.

Just as the young man was about to leave, Ustadji raised his hand and stopped him.

"Wait" he said and then fell silent again, as if some ideas were beginning to play in his head. Then, after a while, he stood up and said – "Why should you go alone? Come, let's all go together. What should we do just sitting here? Why don't we go and watch those trucks and cars speeding by on the highway! Did you know that some travel as many as thousand or even two thousand miles – it's really thrilling to watch those cars! Don't you think so!"

Many from among the crowd immediately stood up and called out to the others "Come on, come on, lets go!" They said, unable to resist their excitement.

Soon, a group of thirty men collected together, and as the news spread further, a few more came running to join them also.

Seeing the huge crowd about to leave, Ramkhilaon felt worried. "My, my, where shall we go with so many greedy men? Who is going to pay for so many cups of tea?" He asked.

Ustadji raised a hand again and said, "Doesn't matter, let them all come, we'll surely be able to work out something."

Phoolsaria looked at Ramkhelaon and said, "Can't you see Ustadji is inviting us, why are you still arguing with him? Aren't his words of any value?"

It was a procession of people with no special purpose. They seemed to be on way to a sudden picnic, breaking away from their otherwise slow, uneventful lives. At the *Pakki,* one could easily make out that there was a distant city on this side of the highway, and another distant city on the other. It was in one of those directions that the nation's capital lay. And even though it was about twenty five to thirty miles away from here in terms of geographical distance, it was actually very far off.

After reaching the highway, the villagers had to turn right and walk for about half an hour before they were able to locate the Sardar's tea stall. But they found the shutters closed, and it seemed as if this shop had been closed for quite some time.

Dhania beat against his head in remorse and said – "My goodness, how did I forget it? Of course, I had heard that there was some trouble in Amritsar, and I knew that the Sardars have been feeling agitated ever since. In fact, a number of them have even fled the city. This Sardarji – the owner of the tea stall too has been missing since the day Indira Gandhi was shot."

"That's right." A few others joined in recollection. "This shop has remained closed for quite some time now."

A shadow of disappointment fell over the faces that had, till this moment, been lit up with eagerness This surely meant the end of their picnic! What a pity, hadn't Ustadji himself invited them to tea, today!

"Doesn't matter." Said Ustadji, "So what if this shop is closed, there are still others, aren't there! Come on, lets go!"

"Where else can we go Ustadji?" Ramkhelaon asked. "The more you keep moving forward, the more you'll be nearing the city, and of course, the tea is costlier there. Besides we are not even properly dressed, and are barefoot ... they'll definitely not let us in!"

In the meantime, a few others had also stopped. They knew

that they could stand and have tea at a wayside stall, but why would a more sophisticated 'shop' let them in?

"Is it the people who drink tea, or is it their shirt and shoes, tell me?" Ustadji asked, as a smile flashed across his face. It was as if another naughty idea had struck him. He took out the newspaper from his pocket, rolled it and kissed it twice. Then he turned to the others and said – "Come on, I am going to treat you to tea at the Taj Mahal today."

Ustadji often said things that made no sense. What on earth was this Taj Mahal? People stared at each other in silent curiosity.

Dhania, who always behaved as if he knew everything, said, "I know. The Taj Mahal is actually a grand palace that belonged to the Badshah. I remember seeing its photo on a calendar in the contractor's house."

"That's right." Ustadji said. "Have you heard of Badshah Akbar? You haven't! Badshah Akbar's grandson built this spacious house for his queen. It is painted as white as this sunlight. It is simply exquisite!"

"Why should we go there?" Someone from the crowd joked. "Has the Badshah sent us an invitation?"

"But the age of the Badshahas and Begums is long over." Dhania said. "They no longer exist. Don't you know even that?"

"Then the ministers must surely be living there with their wives now, isn't it?"

"No, it's a public monument. Ordinary people like us can go there." Ustadji said.

But this wasn't enough to dispel the doubts from peoples' minds. Who knew how far the monument was! What would it cost to have tea there? When would they get to return home?

Ustadji smiled back naughtily. He fished out a hundred rupee note from his pocket and waved it in front of his nose. How amazing indeed! How could a hundred rupee note emerge from that tattered robe? Did this man know some kind of magic?

"What was that you showed us Ustadiji? Where did you get it from?" People cried out in surprise.

"Why, did you think I was just a useless fellow? I earned that as an award for my singing."

The tension that had been growing suddenly disappeared and people laughed aloud. It wasn't possible to believe that someone could actually have paid the Ustadji for his singing. But at the same time, the hundred rupee note that he showed them was a genuine one – it hadn't vanished yet!

Dhania turned to Ustadji and said, "Are you planning to spend that money on us!"

"I don't save money, I earned it at one go and am ready to blow it up in a day!"

"Then why don't you do something else – after all its a lot of money. Why use it just to have tea? Why not make an offering in some temple?"

"That's ridiculous! The only worship I believe in is satisfying my appetite, that's all!"

"Why don't you listen to me, Ustadji! Make an offering of a goat or a buffalo to the Gods, then we can all eat the meat!

"Can you buy a lamb or a buffalo for hundred rupees! At the most you can get only a mouse or two!"

"My husband always talks nonsense." Phoolsaria said, interrupting Dhania. "Let us not discuss about eating meat and all that. I am sure we will get to taste it at least once or twice more, if we live. Now I just want to go and have tea at the *Hawa Mahal* or whatever *Mahal* the Ustadji was just talking about."

A few others also joined in. There was no need to hurry back home, so the group of villagers kept moving towards the *rajdhani*.

After a while, they saw a man pass, playing a small drum. He was accompanied by a rather sickly looking bear and two monkeys. Ustadji stepped forward, placed a hand on the man's shoulder, and asked. "Where are you going my friend?"

It was clear that the man knew Ustadji. He looked up and said, "I don't follow any particular direction. I let my heart direct me to wherever it wants! But where are you off to with this big group of people?"

"We are going somewhere to have tea, why don't you come along too? It's really nice that we found you."

"You mean all these people are going to have just some tea?"

"Why don't you come, I'll treat you to some really good tea – the like of which you have never had in your life."

"Yes, yes, we are all going to have tea at the Taj Mahal." Someone shouted from the back.

The bear-man suddenly stopped, surprised. He brushed aside Ustadji's hand from his shoulder and stared into his eyes. He was not a man who got easily swayed by the words of other people.

"What did that man say about the Taj Mahal? Where are you all going to have tea? He asked.

"Oh, we are going to the Taj Mahal." Ustadji answered, smiling naughtily.

"Do you take me to be, a fool? Am I not aware of what the Taj Mahal is? I know that its very, very far from here and that this direction that you have taken actually leads to the *rajdhani*."

"Come on my friend, come with us. Didn't you say that you had no fixed destination in your mind? Then why not come with us?"

"Are you planning to walk all the way to the *rajdhani*? It's much too far, not only men but even these animals of mine would tire if they had to walk all that distance."

"In that case, we have to make some other plans."

Three trucks were going down the other side of the road. Ustadji quickly went and stood in the middle of the road, spreading his hands out on both sides. A few others in the group also followed suit. Had it been only an individual or two, the trucks would have surely driven past, maybe even crushing them under their wheels; such were indeed the practices on these roads. But in this case it was a large group of people, about forty, obstructing the road, so the drivers were forced to apply the brakes.

All three trucks were carrying goats. The drivers got down, wondering who these people were. Were they collecting donation on behalf of some political party?

Phoolsaria had never seen such a sight. "Ustadji, where are they carrying all these goats?"

"To the rajdhani, where people are always hungry!" Ustadji replied. "That is why they pick up the best of the goats, chicken, cows, fish, milk and everything else from the villages. They even pick up women!"

"Do they eat them up also?"

"Ha, ha, ha! Don't worry Phoolsaria, with so many of us here, nobody will be able to gobble you up."

Then Ustadji moved forward to where the truck-drivers stood, folded his hands and said.

"My brothers, my friends, will you please give us a lift upto the rajdhani?"

The drivers were rather relieved to hear the request. Indeed, it wouldn't have been possible to move ahead, if these people had kept obstructing the road. It would have taken at least twenty four hours for the police to come and clear it, and that would have proved very expensive. Besides, these people hadn't really asked for anything – not even a donation.

The drivers initially expressed some hesitation about being able to accommodate all of them, but on second thoughts they decided to find out if they were willing to pay for the ride. Ustadji immediately replied that there wouldn't be any problem with accommodating them, his people were ready sit with the goats on their lap. He also said that they wouldn't be able to offer any money for the ride, but once they reached the city, he could treat them to tea.

This seemed agreeable to the drivers, but they were not willing to take the bear and the monkeys in their trucks. The Ustadji was of course quick to reassure them.

"Have you seen what this poor bear looks like?" He asked. "It's smaller than any of those goats, not frightening enough to scare anybody. Come on, come on, let's not delay any more!"

Phoolsaria and the other women in the group felt very happy. It was such a lovely change in their otherwise routine life. Who else but Ustadji could have come up with such a brilliant idea? They didn't even know where they were all heading for, but that didn't really matter, did it?

As the trucks moved on, a few among the party began to sing aloud, while others clapped in joy. Oh, this was such fun! Ever since Ustadji had come up with that magical idea of having tea, the whole day had changed for all of them!

As the city lights began to be seen in the distance, the villagers stared with abated breath. Was this a fairy land? Even the clouds seemed to hang much lower here! Of course a few of them had visited the *rajdhani* earlier, but then they had come as labourers. This trip was entirely different. It seemed as if they were now on their way to conquer the place.

Phoolsaria couldn't control her excitement. She turned to Ustadji and said, "Isn't the Taj Mahal the biggest building in this area? Can we see it from here?"

"Of course you will, in due time. And then it's bright white colour will simply dazzle your eyes, Phoosaria!"

The trucks stopped near the borders and asked the people to get off. They were not allowed to enter the city, so they had to refuse Ustadji's offer of tea. As they sped away, Ustadji and his group began to walk through what seemed to them a fairy land. Goodness, there were so many different types of cars on the streets and so many policemen standing around. If only Ustadji had informed them of his plan earlier, they would have certainly come in their best clothes! Suddenly, Phoolsaria remembered that beautiful rose patterned saree that she had left at home, did it really make any sense to be dressed in this yellow one that was not only very ordinary but also torn?

Ustadji kept stopping from time to time, asking the passers by something. He didn't hesitate to talk to the policemen also – brave man that he was! So they walked on. Who knew how many roads they must have crossed? Finally, at one point of time, Ustadji asked them to stop. Then, pointing to the huge building in front of him, he said – "There it is – the Taj Mahal!"

As they stared at the building, many of them couldn't hide their disappointment. Hadn't it belonged to the *badshahs* and *begums*! Shouldn't it have been something absolutely different, much more magnificent? Where was that much awaited palace of the kings and queens? True, this was a huge building, but hadn't they seen many such buildings on their way here? In fact some of those had been even bigger. Besides, this wasn't even as white and bright as the sun!

"This one!" Dhania asked, unable to hide a note of disappointment.

The bear-man wasn't convinced either. He turned to Ustadji and said "Why are you joking with us? How can this be the Taj Mahal? This is only a hotel."

"Of course it is." Ustadji replied. "Where else other than a hotel can one get to drink tea?"

"Why didn't you say that earlier?"

"Had I done so, it would have only made my friends more nervous. But I haven't really lied. This hotel is indeed known as the Taj Mahal Hotel. You can go and ask that durwan if you don't believe me."

Ustadji was right. On hearing that this was actually a hotel, the villagers grew nervous True, Ustadji had shown them the hundred rupee note that he had, and that wasn't really a small sum, but it wasn't all that much either. It couldn't fetch even a buffalo or a goat! Was it possible to have a cup of tea with it in such a high-class hotel? And even if it was possible, would the authorities let people like them step in?

The head durwan of the hotel truly resembled the erstwhile *nawab-badshahs*. Dressed in a silk vest, with a neatly tied turban on his head, he sported a large moustache, quite regal looking. To add to that royal look, he even held a small wand-like stick with a brass knob that shone like gold. Seeing so many people who looked like beggars standing in tattered clothes and bare feet, he broke into a roar. "Get out, get out at once." He ordered.

The sound of that thunderous voice was enough to deflate the villagers' spirits and they looked around for cover, trying to hide behind each other's back. But Ustadji was not to be deterred. He moved forward till he stood facing the head durwan. Then without any hesitation, he placed a friendly hand on the man's silk-jacketed chest, smiled a little and said, "We are clients, brother, we are all clients here. We will pay and eat. How can you send us back?"

But the Head Durwan wouldn't yield. "Get out, get out, clear the gates." He kept repeating.

While all this was going on, a commotion had already started inside the hotel. Everyone starting from the junior manager to the head stewart was running around looking worried, trying to find out what this trouble was all about, and how it could be tackled. Even though the hotel had its own security guards, the police were called. After all, there were so many *sahibs*, and *memsahibs* and so many important businessmen staying here. And they had to be protected. What had the hotel management possibly done that had made so many thugs and wicked people from the village *gherao* them?

The junior manager looked down from the first floor balcony and ordered the guards and policemen. "Throw them out, clear the gates at once."

Ustadji looked up and shouted back. "What are you saying manager *sahib*? Why are you blabbering in English? Were you born of an English father? But your complexion is just like mine, isn't it?"

The manager didn't pay any heed to his words. He continued to speak, undeterred. "Get out from here, all of you and don't make so much noise." He ordered. "If you don't listen to me, the police will come and push you out this very minute. Do you hear me?"

"What strange words you speak, manager *saab*?" Ustadji continued. " Do you know that you are driving away your clients? I have read our Constitution, it doesn't mention anywhere that people need to have shoes on in order to enter a hotel. We'll pay for the food that we eat, and that's all that's needed."

"You will not be allowed to eat here. Go and find some other hotel."

"Why can we not be allowed here? Do you ask all your

customers to prove that they have enough money before letting them in? The Constitution doesn't demand that either."

The junior manager quickly moved away to contact a police booth bigger than the earlier one.

In the split of a second, several police vans and their mighty-looking officers arrived on the scene. Seeing so many policemen, the villagers got very scared and did not know where to go. Huddled together in fear, they began to wail helplessly, "What did you do Ustadji? We came all this way trusting your words and now, instead of tea, you are planning to have us beaten up. If the police lock us up in jail, then what will happen to our work in the fields? What will our children eat?"

Snatching the drum from the bear-man's hands, Ustadji shook it into a loud beat and said, "Listen brothers and sisters, a man's promise is as firm and precious as an elephant's tusk. I have promised to treat you to tea at the Taj Mahal hotel, the kind of tea that you have never tasted before. Those of you who are cowards go back. And those of you who believe me, stay by my side."

A hushed murmur arose for a second, but it died immediately. Nobody, not even one of his companions moved back. After all, who would like to be called a coward? Ustadji was well-meaning, surely he wouldn't put them in danger deliberately. This was possibly another comic occasion like that earlier one when they had confined the bridge contractor under the date-palm!

Just then, one of the police officers stepped forward and asked Ustadji, "Are you their leader? Step over this side, I need to talk to you."

"What can I discuss with a small officer like you?" Ustadji said, undaunted. "Go call your Commissioner, or else the Prime Minister. I can only talk to people who have read the Constitution of our country."

Such defiance from an unimportant man! The police officer fumed. Had this been somewhere in the suburbs, he would have beaten them up and taught them a lesson they would never forget. It wouldn't have mattered even if two or three of them died in the process. But this was after all the capital, with hundreds of embassies and so many journalists hanging around, nobody knew what the consequences might be. In fact, The Home Minister could even order an immediate suspension!

So, the head of the police had a second round of discussion with the hotel managers. There was only one way of ending this trouble. These beggars were only spoiling the ambience of the garden, so the sooner they could be got rid of, the better.

This time, the senior manager came over to the balcony and addressed the people. "Alright, since all of you have come to have tea here, the hotel management has decided they will offer you tea free of cost, as a gesture of goodwill. But first, go and stand outside the gate, the tea will be sent there."

At last the peoples' faces lit up in joy. So, Ustadji had really triumphed and now they would get to drink the promised tea.

But Ustadji raised a hand and stopped them. Then he looked at the manager and said in a taunting manner, "Rubbish! Are we beggars that we will have to drink our tea, standing on the roadside? We are free citizens of this country, and we shall pay for whatever we eat. But of course, we shall first sit on proper chairs, rest our elbows on the table and then drink that tea."

Then he called out to his people." Come on, come on, lets' get in."

Immediately, everybody rushed in, with Ustadji leading the way. The tables inside were all occupied by sahibs and memsahibs from many foreign countries, and there were also the brown coloured sahibs dressed in western clothes. Seeing so many people looking like beggars rush into the room, they screamed, and began to push and shove each other out. Within a short time, the villagers occupied all the chairs.

Ustdaji turned to Dhania and said – "So, did you see what happened? Now, give me a *bidi*!"

Everybody hailed their brave leader.

After a while, a hotel stewart wearing a black bow tie came to their table, and in a voice that sounded rather curt said, "Listen, you want to drink tea – that's alright, we'll serve you tea. But according to our rules we cannot allow people with monkeys and bears. So, please go and leave them outside."

No sooner had the stewart finished, Ustadji flashed out a newspaper from his pocket, and held open the front page. "Whose picture is this – can you see? Look carefully, do you recognise it?"

It was the picture of a bear, and indeed on the very first page!

Ustadji turned to his people and said – "Listen brothers and sisters, the bear that you see in this photograph is actually owned by this hotel. Yes, I am telling you the truth. It's all written in the newspaper. This hotel has sent this bear to France where it will be made to perform at various hotels. I don't lie, I am telling the truth, see everything is written here. If this hotel can send its bear to other hotels, then why can't we bring our own bears here? For sure, we can!"

Everybody laughed out and expressed their support in Ustadji's favour. If a bear could be allowed to enter foreign hotels, why couldn't it enter one here?

By now, the police were already trying to contact the Home Minister over telephone, but he wasn't available. There was no one to instruct them as to what weapons they should resort to, to counter the present situation – sticks, tear gas, or bullets? Indeed it would be better to treat them to their desired tea and have done with it!

There were several expensive ash trays and flower vases lying on the tables! And these thugs were surely going to steal them! So the manager immediately sent bearers to remove the table accessories. But Ustadji was not one to withstand this insult. He caught one of the bearers, and said – "Listen, just because you are serving wealthy men, have your antecedents changed? Did your father and brothers never work in the fields at some point of time? Can you recognise us? Where does the Constitution say that one can shake off only the ash from a cigarette and not from a bidi in a hotel? Don't try to teach me all that!"

Then with a flick of his thumb, he called out to the stewart and said, – "Here, bring me that card which has the names of all the items and their prices written on it!"

From the many menu cards that were lying on the tables, one was handed to Ustadji. He pretended to read it seriously, and as his eyes moved down the page, he kept cursing to himself, "Thieves, dacoits all! Just for a piece of dry chicken they charge hundred and fifty rupees! For a plate of nuts – it's twenty five rupees! Robbers, cheats!" And then changing his tone, he said, "No, we will only have tea. Go, get us forty cups of tea."

A couple of foreigners carrying cameras were peeping curiously from behind the inner door. Ustadji called out to them in Hindi, "Come here, come here, come and take your photographs!"

Then he brought forward a sickly, impoverished looking man called Dukhiram from his group, and stood him right in front of the waiting cameras. "Take this man's photo." He said to the men standing behind the cameras. "Our own Rajivji has gone to France and Africa to celebrate. He has carried the marble statues from our museums to introduce our country to them. But those are all representatives of erstwhile India. Look at this man – Dukhiram! This is the India of today!"

But before the cameras could click, the police walked in and moved away the foreigners saying that they were not allowed to take photographs as and when they wanted. Besides, who knew when violence might be sparked off Those men were now thumping the tables and joking among themselves. Why were the bearers delaying in bringing the tea?

After a while, the tea was brought in big pots. As soon as the bearer began to pour it into cups, Ustadji stopped him and asked him to leave. Then he turned to Phoolsaria and said –

"*Devi* Phoolsaria, you alone are the begum of this Taj Mahal today. Why don't you serve us tea with your own hands?"

After everybody had got a cup, they began to sip it noisily.

"It's really nice! What a fine fragrance, we have never tasted such tea, ever! You deserve praise, Ustadji, you really do." They were overwhelmed!

It was only Phoolsaria who had tears in her eyes. Ustadji was surprised. "What is it Phoolsaria, why are you crying? What are you feeling sad for?"

In a voice choked with emotion, Phoolsaria said, "I am feeling very happy Ustadji. I really am. I am just an ordinary woman, and no one has ever given me such honour before, never."

"Of course, it's only because you have served tea with your own hands that there's such a beautiful fragrance, and that is also why it tastes so sweet. Isn't that right, what do you all say?"

Everybody agreed.

The bear man suddenly said, "Oh, oh, you drank up all the tea, without giving a drop to these monkeys and this bear?"

Indeed, it was a oversight, they had made a terrible mistake. Everybody poured out a little from their own cups on to a plate, and offered it to the animals sitting on the floor, by their side.

The sickly bear's eyes lit up as it sipped tea from the plate. After all he had never tasted such a beautiful thing ever before, it was almost as if he was gaining back his health.

Ustadji clapped in front of the bear and said – "Come on pretty bear, dance, dance. Dance, Munna dance."

Then they all stood around the bear and started clapping joyously.

Blood and Tears
Rakta ebong Asru

Everyone agreed that the boy could take a beating! It wasn't that his body was all that strong, on the other hand he had a frail and tallish frame. His shoulders hunched like a vulture's and his complexion was like the rain filled clouds of monsoon. He never made the slightest sound when slapped or kicked, not even when he was hit with a stick. At times when he fell down after a severe beating, it would seem as if he had fainted, but he would be back on his feet the next minute, as if nothing had happened. His head had cracked so many times, once he even had to tie a bandage round his right hand for two months!

That he was still alive was really surprising!

It was for his capacity to tolerate such a beating, that people had got to know of Bangshi's name. Out of the five dacoits who had once attacked Matigada, two had fled, but the rest had been beaten to death. It had taken quite some time for the story to be spread in various ways by various people. In fact someone had even said that had Bangshi been one of those dacoits, then nothing much would have happened, and he would have easily stood up again.

Those who still had not heard of Bangshi wondered who he was. For others – he was 'that lad from Kuchilapara' whom nobody had ever seen shed a tear, not even if his entire body bled profusely! Indeed, there are some people in this world who do not seem to have tears in them. Or maybe their tears mingle with their blood, who knows!

The fact that Bangshi often got beaten up had of course its own reasons. He wasn't used to obeying orders or following any social custom, not even the ones that existed within his own world. Actually, his parents had named him Bangshidhari. But he had been beaten up by his teacher once because of this name. Apparently, he didn't deserve such a name, at the most, he could only be called "Bangshi" and nothing more, his teacher had said!

There is no set pattern which makes people keep moving from one place to another. Specially those who have never put an iron shaft on their land, whose temporary homes keep blowing off time and again in cyclones, they always seem to drift away like withered leaves caught in the midst of a storm.

It was possibly in this manner, that Bangshi's grandfather, Shanichari Banshua had migrated from his village in Chappra zilla to Tripura. Had he come alone or as part of a group? Of course, there was no indication to suggest that there were others with him. Had he come in search of a living? In that case, why did he not move to a bigger city like Agartala or Udaipur, instead of choosing a distant, inaccessible mountainous village like this?

Of course, this village was not all that small now. Many people from Kumilla had come and spread out all over Tripura They had engaged themselves in farming, opened up shops and some had even become landlords. Earlier this place was known as Makuria, but now it had quite an ostentatious name – Kumarnagar. Even though the village was small in size, it had many facilities that included a stationary store, a grocery shop, and a sweet shop. It even had a small club for the local youth called "*Tarun Sangha.*" Besides these, there was also a two storeyed house of the Chatterjees who were the local landlords. This was known as the 'smaller palace.'

When a village gradually changes into a city, it throws up the demand for men in various professions, like blacksmiths, potters, carpenters, school teachers, priests and others. In more recent times, there is also a need for electricians, political leaders, and even dealers in illicit liquor. Shanichari Banshua of Bihar was a scavenger by profession. It is a known fact that with the increasing size of a city, the need for scavengers also increases. But why didn't Shanichari Banshua move to Calcutta? After all, for large cities like Calcutta, the responsibility of garbage cleaning lay with the Bihari scavengers. The fact that instead of joining people from his native village, Shanichari had come all this way to Tripura, was probably because he had wanted to change his profession.

Apart from cleaning drains and toilets, Shanichari was good at making certain handicrafts. He could make various kinds of baskets, winnowing platters and mattresses out of cane. Indeed, he was called Banshua because of his expertise in working with *bansh*. Different varieties of bamboo were available in Tripura, and things made out of those were quite attractive.

Even though the fact that Shanichari belonged to the scavenger class was not explicitly written over him, people could easily recognize him as one. Such men spread the information themselves. As if it was their eternal fate to remain fallen, and untouchable in society, and a great sin to conceal their cast identities!

Whenever a stranger arrives at a place, his identity and purpose of visit arouses suspicion among the local people. Shanichari had migrated along with his family, as a hawker selling baskets. But his true identity didn't remain unknown for long.

One day, Shanichari's wife Dhania went to bathe in the nearby pond. It was a large pond, where people swam from early morning to late hours of evening. On that very first day, Dhania had seen a man standing knee-deep in the waters, with his face turned to the skies, and his hands joined in prayer. He wore the sacred thread and was uttering Sanskrit chants. Her heart had frozen in fear. Was that man a Brahmin? After all, one couldn't wear those sacred threads unless one was a Brahmin, and moreover he was clearly chanting Sanskrit mantras. Had she really stepped into the same waters as him? This would surely spell evil for her husband and children!

Dhania could have easily slithered past, without letting anyone know. But one couldn't learn such tactics without living in a city. She had sat down in true rustic simplicity and honesty and burst into tears, blaming her own fate. She had committed a sin unknowingly! She remembered that back in her own village Chapra, her father in law's brother had once touched a priest inadvertently. Even though he had afterwards rolled in dust and begged for pardon, the priest had not forgiven him. Wasn't it because of the priest's curse that the man's elder son had died soon after, spitting blood?

Seeing Dhania in tears, the other women gathered around her in curiosity. They began to cross examine her and soon got to know everything. All eyebrows lifted in disbelief! This woman was a sweeper's wife, and yet, she had dared to step into the same waters with the brahmins and kayasthas! What greater sin could she have committed!

But nobody had beaten her up that day. Instead, a middle aged woman had spoken to her kindly, "Why are you sitting here and shedding tears, you ill fated daughter? She had said. "You have sinned without knowing! Doesn't matter, just get away from here quickly, and don't tell anyone about this. Remember, if the men here ever get to know, they will surely set your house on fire!"

Actually, the real problem lay with the pond. Hadn't its waters become unholy from the profane touch of a sweeper's wife! This was the largest lake in Kumarnagar. Of course there was another lake within the boundaries of the palace that belonged to the younger *zamindar*, but not everybody could use it, in fact most people used this pond. Even though the news hadn't spread, those women who heard of this sacrilegious event couldn't let their husbands and children bathe in these waters any more. So, what was the way out? Even if one killed that low-caste female now, it wouldn't really help!

Finally, a way out was found. Nanibala, whose husband was the priest in charge of the Zamindar's temple, also bathed in these waters. That day Nanibala wasn't present at the ghats, so the other women went and informed her of this disastrous event. Nanibala was in the habit of bathing three times a day, she too would have to use the same pond later, so she had her own interest in this matter. After racking her brains hard, she came up with a plan. If a few drops of Ganga water could be poured into the pond now, it would surely become pure again. After all, just a few drops of the holy water could save even the worst of sinners!

But where would one get Ganga water from? Tripura didn't have any tributary of the river flowing through it. The Ganga was far off. Yet, its waters were needed for the social and religious rites practised by the Hindus living here. In fact many people who lived here hadn't seen Bengal at all. If anyone ever went to Kolkata or Malda, he would carry back some bottles of Ganga water with him. Kerosene bottles filled with Ganga water were even sold in Agartala at a high price of ten rupees each, with a label of the Seth company certifying the purity of its contents.

Nanibala knew that a few bottles of Ganga water were always preserved at the royal temple. But being a very rare and expensive item, people spent it in measured doses, and kept a count of the bottles used. In fact even when it was used by the priest for sprinkling the *Shanti jal* at the end of the Durga Puja, hardly a drop or two would land on the bowed heads of the people standing around.

Would it be all right then to ask the priest for some Ganga water now? One would have to think well and decide. Who knew how he would react if he got to know the truth. Maybe he would create a lot of noise and demand that an elaborate worship be held as a penance for that sacrilegious act of Dhania's.

After all Nanibala knew her husband well. And if that happened, would anyone spare that foolish sweeper woman who was the source of all this trouble? The over enthusiasts would probably even burn her up!

No, it was better to complete the job secretly. Nanibala managed to steal a bottle of Ganga water from the temple and not seeing anybody around, began to pour the contents into the pond till half a bottle remained. The head clerk usually maintained an account of the bottles in his account register. Anyway, half a bottle was enough for this purpose! Who would ever get to know if she now filled up the bottle with some water and kept it back in its place? Of course it wouldn't be right to fill it up with completely adulterated water. If she could fill the bottle with water from the same pond where she had just poured the Ganga water, then surely all possible vices would get corrected. So, the bottle was returned to the shelf, as full as it initially was!

Shanichari Banshua was a quiet and composed man. After his true identity got revealed, he was called to clean up the toilets in the smaller palace, but he didn't protest. It was an unpaid job that he had to do in lieu of a piece of land that was given to him out of the zamindari quota, for building a house. He cleaned toilets and garbage in other homes also. But he had not given up making bamboo handicrafts. After all bamboo was very cheap here, and he was really very deft at it.

Every Tuesday, at the local market, Shanichari would sit a little away from the other vendors and spread out the earthen jars that he had made. The Brahmins and Kayasthas who knew him, never bought his goods. Yet his craft sold well. The mountain tribals and Muslims were his main customers. On some days, wholesalers would even buy off the entire lot. They would later sell them in cities, and then the Brahmins and Kayasthas in those places would buy goods made by the same 'untouchable' Shanichari Banshua! It wasn't sacrilegious to buy them unknowingly! There are many Brahmins who don't eat anything that has been touched by any member of the lower castes, but they eat rice prepared from the paddy that is grown on land owned by the same farmers. After all, how could they ever know which paddy was coming from whose land?

The extra money that Shanichari made from selling his bamoo ware, was what he used for feeding his wife and children. Actually, he was somewhat better off than the others of his caste.

Maybe, it was because of this that he had trained his son Budhia in the art of bamboo-craft right from a young age. Like the Brahmins, and Kayasthas, the upper caste Hindus too could change their professions at their will, but it wasn't possible for the lower castes to do so. They weren't even allowed to enter the mainstream of society, and had to remain outside all major activities. So, some time later, Budhilal too settled down into the same vocation as his father, cleaning toilets in the smaller palace, and selling bamboo-ware at the same place in Manglahat.

But even if someone like Budhilal could not change his profession, he could change his name. That small freedom was at least there. But he wouldn't get a surname. People who live at the fringe of society never have a surname. Budhilal was known as Budhan Banshdhani. Of course, they were not Beharis anymore, they had to be Bengalis.

Budhan Banshdhani spent a peaceful life without any special event. He had married, given birth to a son and four daughters, and saved for their marriages. His son had a brush with death when only a year old, but he had finally survived due to Lord Ladlimohan's grace. Budhan had, in due course of time, trained him in the art of bamboo craft. The young boy seemed to have picked up the craft rather fast. He could scrape off bamboo poles and roll them out to make a mat. He was so good at weaving those mats, that they seemed like soft strings.

What it implied was that this family was connected with the art of bamboo work for three generations. In that respect, it was not all that irrelevant for Budhan Banshdhani's son to be called Bangshi. But, Bangshidhari? Did his father or grandfather know the meaning of that word? Wasn't that the reason why a school teacher had once threatened him – "If you ever utter that name again, I will beat you with a shoe." He had warned.

Two

For quite some time, a school founded by the zamindars had been started in the village. Children from decent homes went to that school. The local government had also started a school in Kumarnagar sometime back. As caste distinction was not an issue for the government, anybody could be admitted to that school. No fee was charged either, students had to pay only for their books and pencils, nothing else.

Shanichari was still alive and it was because of his interest and encouragement that Bangshi was sent to the government school. In his long life, Shanichari had noticed that people who were educated wielded more power in society than the rich. It was they who ruled the government. Those who were educated became judges and magistrates and they could even send rich people to jail! He had heard that someone by the name of Jagjivan Ram from a *chamar* family like his, had got educated and earned himself the respectable title of '*Babu*'. Couldn't some one from his own family become a *Babu* also?

In the meantime, having spread over three generations, Budhan's family had grown in size, and together with his grandchildren they were now seventeen members in all. At one time, Budhan Bansdhani fell ill, but since the garbage and sanitary needs of the zamindar's and other aristocratic homes couldn't be kept waiting, Bangshi, who was only nine years old then, had been sent with a broom to clean up the refuse. After a few days, one of Budhan's sons in law volunteered to do the job. This work was indeed better than his earlier job of looking after a cow in some other house, mainly because in some homes, sweepers were at least offered stale food, and also a short *dhoti* at the time of the Pujas!

In spite of being admitted to school, Bangshi couldn't make much of it. Was it possible to bring about such changes in just one generation? It was difficult for him to concentrate or even follow the maths that his school teachers taught. And besides, there was the usual scuffle among fellow mates also. Young boys generally seem to be rather cruel, their sense of morality doesn't quite develop before their adolescence. In this case too, the boys in his class didn't seem to forget even for a moment, that Bangshi was a low caste! He was kept away from everybody's touch, and made to sit on the last bench in the classroom. Yet, if he ever came physically in contact with someone, then they would attack him collectively, and beat him up severely, at times even injuring him. Those who did not want to touch him otherwise, didn't find it sacrilegious to touch him while beating him. Yet this boy was so foolish, so unaware of self defence, that at times he would even derive fun by touching someone purposely, and then getting beaten up later on. As if he truly enjoyed getting thrashed. On the contrary, he never hit anyone on his part, possibly because boys like him knew that they were born only to be beaten up, without a right to protest. The slightest effort towards any kind of retaliation could end in his losing even his own life!

It was really difficult to analyze this trait of Bangshi's. Why did he incite such suffering on himself?. Why did he keep entering sweet shops in spite of being forbidden repeatedly? He had been told time and again that even if he had the money, he should wait outside the shop, that he should keep aside his coins carefully and ensure that he receive his packet of sweets from the shopkeeper's hands, without as much as even touching him. These were social customs! In spite of that, if he ever entered the shop, for the first time he would be let off with a mild reprimand, but if he repeated that offence again, then obviously he would have to suffer getting beaten up by at least a fan that was used for lighting ovens. Again, why did he always like to sit at the back of horse-drawn carriages? Was it only to get lashed by the driver's whip? The pond where his grandmother had once dipped into and yet been let off without being burnt alive, if he tried to wash his feet in the same waters today secretly, why would he be pardoned, he would obviously be punished!

One day, Bangshi had entered the Shiva temple that belonged to the Zamindars, and even after being spied by the priest he had not run away. It would be natural to assume that he might have entered the temple to steal something. After all it was only these low caste people who became petty thieves. In fact, whenever there was a major burglary in any part of the village, the police would always go searching in the slums as their first step of investigation. It was after he was caught red-handed in the temple that day, that he had been beaten up severely until one of his hands broke.

Even when Bangshi got beaten up by other boys, the teachers never sympathized with him. Of course, had he been an intelligent student, maybe one of the best boys in class, matters could have been different. But, he always played truant, and was slow and neglectful in his studies. That is why the teachers kept telling him, "Why make such useless efforts? Could a goat be ever used to plough paddy fields? For a blockhead like you, nothing can get inside, not even if pushed with a rivet. Can people like you ever digest food without inhaling the stench from gutters?"

Still, Bangshi had somehow managed to come upto class eight, but he couldn't sit for the scholarship test. That year he found himself in serious trouble with his classmates. One day, Jagmohan, the constable's son, suddenly realised that two of his books were missing. The majority of the boys pointed an accusing finger at Bangshi. Indeed, it could have been the right accusation. After all, it was true that Jagmohan had lost his books, and who other than Bangshi would steal those? Of course, Bangshi had denied vehemently, but then, did a thief ever own up easily? The severity of the beating that followed broke three of his teeth, and his knee got badly injured. The fact that he still did not cry out infuriated his attackers all the more.

After that Bangshi had high fever for ten days. In the meantime the school exams had commenced. Budhan Banshdhani looked at his son and said, "Enough, you don't have to go to school any more."

Even after that incident, the boy found himself in the midst of such self-invited sufferings, several times.

Towards the end of his school career, Bangshi became friends with a few Muslim boys. The tribals from the hills never opposed him, but they usually stopped studying after the fourth or fifth class and were not seen around any longer, in fact they never came this way any more. Whenever Bangshi visited the Muslim localities, he was not chased away. Rather his friend Khaled would welcome him into his house and offer him a seat while his mother served them *muri* and green chillies in two cups. One day she had even served him delicacies like *Shuntki maach and paanta bhatt* and they had relished its spicy tang till they could no longer bear it, and till it made them roll over on the floor, sending everybody at home into fits of laughter —"Why can't you eat spicy food?" Khaled had asked him. "Don't you know, it helps keep the body strong?"

After he developed a kind of sensibility, there was one question which constantly bothered Bangshi. He knew that Khaled was a Muslim and he Bangshi, was a Hindu, then why was it that Khaled never considered him an untouchable, while the Hindus shooed him off with contempt? Could it then be that he was not really a Hindu?

After leaving school, Bangshi started spending most of his time in the Muslim locality. Khaled had an uncle named Mushirul who was not all that old, maybe just five years older than them.

It was this man who later brought about a complete change in Bangshi's life.

Since his brother in law Bashir had taken over the charge of cleaning toilets in the zamindar's house, Bangshi didn't have to do that work any more. It was only if Bashir ever fell sick, that he was needed to do that. On the whole, Bangshi was relieved from the duty of going out with a broom every morning. Instead, he started making more baskets and mats, and attended the local markets regularly, but it still left him with a lot of free time, and he began to visit Mushirul off and on.

Mushirul was a very handsome man, there was a certain beauty in his physique. He bore a strong resemblance to the person who had enacted the role of Akbar's son Selim, in a play that Bangshi had once seen. He had a well trimmed beard, and his hair fell in locks. He was always clad in a lungi and an ordinary shirt, and never wore a kurta and pyjama. He smoked a bidi very often. Not yet married, he lived alone in a small house next to Khaled's.

This man – Mushirul seemed to be a magician. If you ever gave him some clay, then he could, within a flick of a second, shape a bird or a rabbit from it. He could make anything that one wanted, be it a monkey, a lotus or even a ghost. He seemed to have everything at the tip of his fingers. In fact, the first day that Bangshi had seen this ability of Mushirul's, he had felt absolutely enchanted. It was really surprising to see how a scoop of shapeless mud got transformed into so many different forms by the sheer touch of his fingers. Could such beauty be lying dormant within the mud then? Though the initial mould of clay was silent, the parrot or the dog that Mushirul shaped it into, always seemed, as if it would make a sound any moment!

Just as Bangshi himself made baskets and mats, and then sold them in the market, Mushirul too earned a living by making glasses, and cups from clay. Of course he didn't have the right provisions to bake the clay in his own house, he sent it to Shovan Mollah's house. He made clay dolls for his own interest. He kept making and breaking them. Or maybe he would first mould the clay into a bird and then re-mould it into a rabbit. Seeing Mushirul at work, Bangshi's eyes seemed to pop out in amazement.

Many a time, little children of the locality would come and ask Mushirul for some dolls to play with, and Mushirul would never disappoint them. He would make small mangoes, bananas, little birds or tiny animals out of the clay. Indeed, what a variety of forms he knew-kings, queens, soldiers, cheroot-smoking sahibs, dagger holding executioners, and so many more. His hands kept moving deftly, the *bidi* stuck between his lips would burn off. His eyes narrowed in concentration, and engrossed in his work, he seemed completely oblivious of everything around him. A cup of half finished tea would remain un-sipped by his side, until he finished the work in hand.

One day Bangshi asked him rather timidly, "Chacha, would you please teach me how to make these dolls?"

"Let me see your hand first." Mushirul had said. After feeling Bangshi's palm by pressing it here and there, he had reassured him, "Yes, it seems quite soft indeed, and the fingers too are slender and long. Yes, you may succeed as a sculptor if you try. It wouldn't have been easy if you had fingers that were kind of chubby, like this nephew of mine – Khaled will never be able to do anything much. But remember, you should never hold a spade or hammer in your hand. And you should never hurt the earth under your feet. Never dig it either. Just pick it up lovingly. And instead of speaking too much you should always try to think more."

At first, Mushirul had taught Bangshi to sculpt some relatively easier things, like tomatos, mangoes and bananas. Later he followed it up with bears, tigers and dogs. In fact to carve out human beings, he had to break the sculpted form many times before starting all over again.

In order to please little children, Mushirul mixed various colours in small earthen urns containing water, and made brushes from jute fibres. He would bring torn bits of cloth from tailors who stitched pillow and blanket covers, using all this to give the dolls a look like real human beings. He had even learnt how to paint and decorate with pieces of cloth. This training of Bangshi's was not completely free of cost, he had to gift his teacher a bundle of *bidis* each time he met him. In fact he even picked up the habit of smoking from Mushirul!

It was while speaking to him once that Bangshi became disillusioned.

The other young men of the village often got together at Mushirul's home. Some of them even smoked opium. In fact they brought locally brewed liquor also. In the midst of it all, work went on. Once, while painting a tiger-doll yellow and black, Bangshi discovered a striking resemblance between the tiger's face and that of, Abani Babu, the landlord. He often saw such resemblances in his own sculpture. A parrot's face seemed just like Kusumdidi's – the Head master's daughter. A rabbit resembled the grocer's son! He remembered the day he had been caught in the zamindar's temple, the zamindar Abani Chatterjee had cursed him much more than thrashing him.

Suddenly remembering that, Bangshi said, rather abruptly, "Tell me Chacha, don't you Muslims have any hierarchy of castes in your society! Then, why is there such a discrimination among us Hindus?

Instead of Mushirul, someone else, possibly a *ganja* addict from among others in the room had snapped back immediately. "That is actually what has spelled ruin for the Hindus! Those rascals even consider us as –"

Khaled said, "Listen Bangshi, it's not that we have all migrated from the Arab country. Maybe our ancestors before our fathers and grandfathers were also Hindus. It's only to save ourselves from being tortured by Hindus that we have adopted the Muslim religion, where everyone is considered as equal."

Mushirul flung the bidi from his lips, threw a quick glance around, and then burst out in anger, "Shut-up. Who said, we are all equal? If I ever go to Kamarujjan Sahib's house, will he give me a cordial welcome and offer me a seat in his living room? He is sure to keep me waiting for hours in the verandah outside! Why did Nasim Begum have her maidservant Munira driven out? Don't we know why? Did they treat us kindly for being Muslims?"

Seeing Mushirul so agitated, someone tried to calm him down with supportive words. "That's right, we too have Shias and Sunnis among us, don't we?"

Continuing in the same tone Mushirul said, "Let's leave aside all that. Actually, you should remember that there are only two castes in this world – the poor and the rich. The powerful and the weak can never be equal, no matter what religion they belong to. Can uncultured and rustic Muslim men like us ever get to eat with rich men like Kamarujjin Sahib?"

"Whatever you may say Chacha, we Muslims don't suffer from those innumerable caste problems like the Hindus." Khaled added, "See, they have so many superstitions and religious taboos! The Brahmins will never touch food cooked by the Kayasthas, will they?"

Mushirul said, "Go and see, even there you will find a barrier between the rich and the poor. Do you remember the priest who was earlier in charge of the temple, and whose elder son was called Sukhendu or something like that? That boy was good at playing football, and I remember one of the Zamindar's daughters had even wanted to marry him. In fact they had met secretly a few times. And what happened then? The girl was sent off to Silchar and that boy Sukhendu – I don't even know whether he is alive now. Even his father, the priest, lost his own land and vanished who knows where. It is the same story everywhere about the rich and the poor."

Three

Mushirul generally used clay to make mangoes, jack fruits, dogs and cats. At times, he even made a few well-known characters from one or two stories. Once, he sculpted a boy and girl and told Bangshi – "See, this is Laila and this one – Majnu. Do you know their story, how they had suffered in love?"

Of course, Mushirul did not preserve those human figures,

he destroyed them as soon as the story was told.

Once, Bangshi went to visit Mushirul after some time, and found that he had made a large female figure. He had dressed her in a saree, stuck strands of hair on her scalp, and was so engrossed in painting her eyes, that for a while he didn't even notice Bangshi.

Bangshi felt enchanted by what he saw. What a beautiful face the statue had, as if truly real. None of the real female faces that he had seen was as beautiful as this!

After a while, he asked, "What is the story of this girl, Chacha?"

Mushirul lit a bidi and then replied rather indifferently, "No, there is no story around her."

Mushirul had not married, and never would either. He seemed to have a hidden scar somewhere deep in his heart, but Bangshi was not quite aware of that.

He said, "Shall I say something, Chacha? Last year the Saraswati idol at the Tarun Sangha Club's Puja had a face just like this. Have you moulded this doll after her?"

Mashirul laughed. "Are you mad? Saraswati is a Hindu goddess, she belongs to you. Being a Muslim, why should I try to sculpt something to resemble her? Our religion forbids us from even making any kind of idol. After all, we don't believe in gods. We are forbidden to make images of human beings also. I make all this just to amuse myself, but I destroy them again."

"If you put a *Veena* in her hands now, she will look exactly like Devi Saraswati!" Bangshi said.

Mashirul said, "No, the hand that holds the Veena is bent in a different way. Even her posture is different. I have seen your Goddess Saraswati from a distance. I can remember everything, after seeing it just once."

Bangshi still pleaded. "Chacha, please do not destroy this completely. Make me an idol of Goddess Saraswati, please I will keep it and worship it in my home."

"But do you have the right to worship? You are a low caste by birth. No one except a Brahmin priest has the right to utter Sanskrit chants during the pujas, and of course, no Brahmin will ever step into your house."

One benefit of having read till class eight was that Bangshi could read books on his own. He had already read abridged versions of the epics – *Ramayana* and the *Mahabharata*. Pictorial books with those stories were sold at the village fair. Luckily, there was no one who ever questioned the buyer as to whether he was a Brahmin or a sweeper or a *Babu* or a so-called uncultured man.

Those who could read books generally learnt to think on their own.

Bangshi said, "I will worship the Goddess on my own, within the four walls of my house. Who can stop me from doing that? I remember hearing a song once,

"Oh Ma Saraswati,

give me knowledge, give me learning,

Let my mind always remain in the path of truth"

... "Please Chacha, make me a Saraswati idol" he pleaded.

"Do you really want it?" Mushirul asked. "Then, let's do something. Why don't you sculpt the swan that is supposed to be at Saraswati's feet? Let me re-mould her hands and we can put a Veena then. What else is supposed to be there at her feet?"

"Books" Bangshi said.

"You take charge of making those little things."

It was as if the inner urge of an artist had inspired Mushirul to create something new.

For about three or four days after that, the two of them continued to work on transforming a certain nameless female figure in clay, into an idol of Goddess Saraswati, as if this was a game of some sort. Just turning around the posture and the hands of the idol resulted in giving it such a different look. Bangshi felt totally amazed!

Like a teacher teaching his student, Mushirul explained, "See, this is how the fingers are to be carved. I am sure you know that no one has fingers of equal length? Even the part below the elbow is slightly longer than the part above, have you noticed?"

All the while, they hadn't the faintest idea of the consequences that such an innocent game could have!

There are some among the human species, who seem peaceful and quiet during the daytime but are dacoits at night. There are also some who seem friendly but turn into enemies as soon as one's back is turned. It was someone like that from among those who came to drink and make merry in Mushirul's house who complained to one of their own patrons about this secret work of art.

Just when the image of Saraswati was almost complete, a group of men, armed with heavy sticks stormed into the room.

According to them, Mushirul had committed a major offence- by making idols. Not only that, he had faulted even further by keeping the idol of a Hindu god in his house.

When everybody cornered Mushirul and started assaulting him, Bangshi cried out helplessly. "Chacha did not make that, it was I who made it." He kept repeating in despair.

But, nobody paid any attention to him.

Battered with the beating, Mushirul pleaded with his attackers, "Please forgive me this one time, I had not realized my mistake, please forgive me. Believe me, I am a true Muslim, I read the *namaaz* ever day."

Of course, there was no question of any forgiveness. A *fatwa* had already been passed on him.

Those who were beating Mushirul did not stop with just a few slaps and beating with sticks. While some held him tightly, one of them hit hard against his right hand till it broke.

The man who had once told Bangshi, "Never hurt the earth, never hold a hammer in the hand that you sculpt idols with", now found his own hand broken into pieces by the blow of a heavy iron rod. Even though Bangshi's heart broke as he watched this barbaric scene, he didn't have the courage to put up any kind of resistance. None of Mushiul's friends dared to protest either.

One of the attackers even tried to destroy the Saraswati idol, but some one else showed a more sensible mind and prevented him, saying, "Don't destroy a Hindu image. It might, on the contrary result in more trouble. Just give it away to this low-caste Hindu boy, instead."

The one who was carrying the rod looked threateningly at Bangshi and said, "Pick up that doll and run. Remember,'ll break your leg if you ever dare come this way again."

It's not very clear as to what happened to Mushirul after that. Some said that he died. Others said that he had walked some seven miles to lodge a complaint at a police station, but that again had added to his offence and brought him further punishment. His home had been set on fire and destroyed completely. Maybe, Mushirul had somehow fled to Bangladesh. Nobody there could get to know of this sacrilege of his. But no matter where he was, he would not be able to use his right hand ever again!

Although Bangshi himself could suffer silently, he was absolutely stunned by the monstrous and loathsome sight of Mashirul's punishment. Day after day, he remained in a daze, without speaking a word to anybody, as if it had all been his fault. After all, Mushirul hadn't wanted to build the Saraswati, had he? Rather it was he – Bangshi who had requested him.

In any case, Mushirul had made a female form, which was also considered as sacrilegious by the Muslim patrons!

The situation then was such that Bangshi couldn't possibly bring the statue home and worship it. He was not in that frame of mind at all. Besides, his father had also felt intimidated by the very idea. "Can we keep images of gods and goddesses in our house?" He had asked. "Wouldn't that amount to committing a sin? After all, we are sweepers who do filthy work, we are impure. If the word spreads round, who knows what trouble it would spell for us! Go and immerse the statue in the river, or just leave it quietly somewhere by the temple at night. Just make sure that no one sees you."

Of course Bangshi had neither thrown the statue in the waters nor left it near the temple. He had hidden it under his cot, away from the world's eyes..

Actually Bangshi was unable to comprehend the gist of all this talk about sins and sinning that he had heard since his childhood. Would everything he did be considered a sin just because he was born into a sweeper's family? Would a temple lose its sanctity if he entered it? Whose loss was it? The temple's or of those who placed offerings at the temple'? The priest had told him that if he ever touched the holy plate, his hands would be afflicted with leprosy. To tell the truth, Bangshi had picked up just one sweet from that plate!.

But those were childhood pranks. Since then he would often check his hands to see if he really got leprosy. He wondered if the priest's words would come true. At least then he could feel certain that all these threats were based on reality, and would never again raise such questions against any kind of blind faith.

After this, Bangshi was beaten up once again, in front of a large gathering. right inside the market

In the meantime, Budhan Bangshi had passed away, but Bangshi didn't have to take up his profession. He was permanently relieved from walking out to work with a broom in hand. Along with bamboo craft, he had also picked up the art of working with cane, and the money he got by selling those helped him run his household. Meanwhile he had also got married to one of his sister's daughters, and was now a father of two.

Bangshi had not given up his habit of making clay dolls. One day he made a few clay fruits, birds and animals, painted them with bright colours and placed them next to his bamboo and cane ware in the market. At the end of the day he found that, they hadn't done badly by way of sales. Actually, a quick glance at those well crafted bananas or brinjals made them seem almost real and children just loved them. Some even bought those to decorate their houses. Again, it was a convenient thing, as per traditional wedding rules, to fool a new son-in-law with these artificial fruits and vegetables. It provided much merriment for the members of the family to see the new bridegroom being fooled into eating the clay fruits!

Unlike Mushirul, Bangshi did not distribute these clay-figurettes among the neighbourhood kids, instead he started making quite a profit from selling them. His economic condition improved gradually, so much so that his wife even bought herself a pair of silver earrings. His son was also admitted to school, but of course, unlike his father, the boy never went to school without a proper dress on.

On Tuesdays, the market generally attracted people from the neighbouring villages. Not all of them knew that Bangshi was a sweeper's son, and so many of them bought goods from him. One day a middle aged woman came and told him, "I see that you make clay statues; can't you make me an idol of Lord Ganesh? I need one very urgently."

"Of course I can." Bangshi replied. "Come and collect it next Tuesday."

Making a Ganesh was actually very easy. The most difficult part of making a human face was carving out the lips and eyes.

The entire expression of a face, be it anger or joy had to be conveyed through the slant of the lips. Of course, making an image of Ganesh was easy, he didn't have any lips. His eyes were also very small. And his bulging tummy could be fashioned even more easily by keeping the sweet-shop owner Golak Das in mind!

But, what should be the price of a clay Ganesh?

After all there was no money paid for the clay, only a few bits of cloth and paint were needed. The birds and fruits-toys were priced at one rupee and eight annas each. Bangshi asked a price of five rupees for the Ganesh. The woman returned on the following Tuesday, and after a little bargaining, took away the idol at a price of four and a half rupees.

Encouraged by this success, Bangshi made a few more Ganesh idols. All of them sold out. He had not known that there was such a demand for them. Then maybe he should try and make statues of a few more gods and goddesses, he thought!

With the Saraswati Puja only a few months away, surely the Saraswati idol would sell very well! Crouching under the bed, Bangshi pulled out that exquisite statue of Saraswati that Mushirul had once made. Even if he couldn't make something as beautiful, he could at least try and imitate it.

The statue was covered in dust and spider webs. As soon as those were cleared, the idol's face regained its glow, it seemed as if the goddess was smiling at him.

The thought of Mushirul brought a pang of sadness to Bangshi's heart. That man had once taught him this craft with his own hands, who knew where his misfortune had dragged him to!

The next week, Bangshi managed to carry two Saraswati idols to the market. The idols were obviously not as exquisite as Mushirul's but they could at least be recognized as goddess Saraswati. Yes, he would gradually improve. He priced the idols at ten rupees each, and they sold instantly.

The potters of Kumarnagar were all Muslims. That is why the statues of the Hindu gods and goddesses had to be brought from the distant city of Kailashnagar. This not only proved to be quite problematic, it meant a greater expenditure also.

A week later, Bangshi carried with him three Saraswatis and five Ganesh idols to the market place. He had worked very hard, day and night to make them. As far as the bamboo and cane products were concerned, there were some other craftsmen also who made those, so he had to often face a stiff competition with them, but who else could offer gods and goddesses at such a cheap price?

Bangshi had invented another novel way of attracting customers. He carried the idols, half finished, to the market, and then painted the eyes and completed the rest, sitting before the public. A large crowd gathered to watch him work. Customers always asked for genuine and fresh goods, and there was no exception in the case of these statues also. They watched the idols being completed before their own eyes. No, these weren't stale products like those available in Kailashnagar, they were freshly made.

The next week, with the Saraswati Puja drawing close, Bangshi carried five Saraswati idols to the market. And it was on that day that trouble started.

Bangshi usually laid out his fare at the back of the market, and that was why the Hindus belonging to the upper class did not come that way. But craftsman who travelled all the way from Kailashnagar or Agartala to sell their own statues of gods, goddesses and clay toys, did not like this prosperity of Bangshi. They went and complained to some power-wielding *babus*, who then set out promptly with Narottam Samanta, the zamindar's rent collector, as their spokesperson.

Even though Naraottam was dressed in trousers and shirt like a modern gentleman, his attitude and behaviour was rather old fashioned. Like his masters, he held a silver-topped stick in his hand.

Surrounded by his men, he came charging at Bangshi. "So, you seem to have become very smart, is it? How dare you make these Saraswati idols?

'I've made them simply because I know how to make them. Take them if you wish, otherwise just leave them." Bangshi replied quietly. He never spoke defiantly with the gentry.

At that moment, he was totally engrossed in painting the eyes of a statue, and was completely oblivious to anything else. In fact, he didn't even raise his eyes to see the man who had uttered the threat.

This defiance on Bangshi's part was too much for Narottam to bear. Infuriated, he said "How dare you! You have crossed even your own limits! What has become of these low castes, now!"

As he spat out the words, he brought down the stick heavily on Bangshi's shoulder. Bangshi folded his hands and begged – "Babu, please forgive me." He kept repeating.

"What are you asking pardon for?" Narottam roared. "Wasn't it you who had entered the temple once? You've not learned a lesson, have you? You're still touching these stautes of Gods and Godesses with that dirty hand of yours?"

Someone from the group said, "Do you think he'll ever learn from this beating? Just destroy all those idols. Break them!"

Bangshi flung himself forward in a vain attempt to shield the Saraswati and Ganesh statues, but he ended up getting even more thrashed, and the statues broke into pieces.

The Muslims who had once attacked Mushirul had not dared to break the Saraswati idol, but there was nothing holding back the Hindus now. In any case, the idols had already lost their sanctity after being touched by a low caste man like Bangshi.

Those who had come to the market gathered around and watched Bangshi getting beaten. It was as if a thief had just been caught. Even who those knew nothing, came and joined in the slapping and kicking.

Bangshi kept lying on the ground for about an hour. On hearing the news some of his relatives came and carried him away. But after they came to know of the incident, they blamed him alone for his plight. Hadn't he become too big for his shoes, they asked!

All the while that he was being thrashed, Bangshi had been thinking of only one thing. It was actually Mushirul's and his own attempts at making a Saraswati that had led to all this trouble. Nothing similar had happened when they had carved a Ganesh. Was it then that Mother Saraswati had got angry with him? Was it that she did not like anybody who was completely dissociated from the world of learning? But Bangshi had studied up to class eight, and, had he not been restrained, he would have qualified in the scholarship exams also. Mushirul was also somewhat literate. At least both of them could read more books than Fatik Sarkhel, the man who came from Kailashnagar to sell clay toys and images in the market.

After a few days, having recovered somewhat, Bangshi went to the market again. After all, he had to earn a living. But, he would now deal only in bamboo and cane products, he wouldn't be selling clay dolls any more. Not even clay mangoes, bananas or brinjals. Who knew what kind of trouble even those could spark off?

But he started on the image of a Sarasawti at home and this time it was on a large scale.

Now there was only one thought in Bangshi's mind. None of the Saraswatis that he had sculped earlier had been as perfect as the one Mushirul had made. Would he not be able to do something like that? Now that he was not going to sell it, there was no need to hurry. Each day he made a little, at times he would stand a little away from the unfinished statue and inspect it carefully. In case he felt dissatisfied with any part, he would destroy it and start afresh. Now the sense of unfulfillment was only his own.

After continuing this process of making and breaking for a month, Bangshi experienced a sense of satisfaction at what he had created. Placing it next to the one that Mushirul had made, he kept examining it from different corners of the room. Could anyone differentiate between the two? In fact, he secretly thought that this time he had possibly excelled over Mushirul's craft.

What was special about his own Saraswati was that her lips and chin seemed to reflect such a look of peaceful joy!

For the next few days, no one could make out why Bangshi moved around looking happy.

But soon afterwards, another thought crept into his mind. A scientist never paused after making an invention, he always moved to the next step. In fact, not being able to progress was itself a failure. A musician too remains engrossed in composing one song after another, a writer keeps inventing new subjects to write about. In much the same way, as if out of some kind of an inner impulse, Bangshi wondered whether he would be able to make a new image on his own! Did he really have that kind of talent?

Then, as if to prove this to himself, he designed an image of Lakshmi. He followed it up with that of a king and queen. After that it was a statue of Kartik riding a peacock, and a soldier holding a gun. Yes, he could make anything he wanted. He didn't need to have a portrait or some other image in front of him; he could visualize one in his own mind. His fingers seemed to have earned that magic, by which they could mould a form out of an ordinary lump of clay. What was merely a lump a while back, now stared back at him through the eyes of a statue. Even day figure could smile! At times, Bangshi felt enchanted by his own achievement!

Of course, he didn't stop here. He knew now that he could make small statuettes, but what about a four-armed goddess Kali? Could he ever make that? It was a challenge he posed to himself.

Why not try and see, his mind answered and he began his work. First, he had to make a structure out of straw and bamboo.

After that he put one, and then two coatings of clay on the basic mould. He could master this art of coating only after several attempts.

Goddess Kali was worshipped in the cremation grounds also. Of course Bangshi did not know whether the low caste undertakers who lived there had the right to touch the Goddess. He would go there next year and find out. Every time he had seen the Kali Puja at the cremation ground, he had trembled with fear. But he didn't feel scared to see this image that he had made with his own hands. The naked, intimidating female figure, with a falchion in one hand, and a bloody severed head in the other! He would have to see a picture to know what else was there in the other two hands. At her feet lay Mahadev, with a hooded snake on his head.

This idol was for himself alone, yet it cost him substantially. Fortunately, he had always been careful about spending money. He was a total teetotaller, the only thing he was addicted to was *bidis*. Even when he had some extra money, he never spent it on buying good clothes. When he was a child, he never wore a sweater even in the cold winter months, he would always wrap a *chadar* around himself. During the summer, he moved around in bare torso and bare feet. As people grow older, they seem to lose their attraction for the little things that they once craved for in their childhood, those that had remained out of their reach then. Bangshi's own children now wore shoes.

After making the statue of Kali, he didn't keep it for long, he destroyed it. But he felt strongly addicted to this challenging art! Could he now make a Durga Ma with all of her ten arms!

Bangshi kept toying with the idea for quite some time. Wasn't he crossing his limits now? Was it possible for him to make the huge statue of Durga Ma all alone? Wouldn't it involve a lot of expenditure, and time? He would never be able to sell these idols in his entire life, nor would he be able to show them in public! And, in any case. He had already proved to himself that he could achieve this. So what was the need for doing anything more?

How many people understand the different levels of a human mind? Bangshi had already decided that he wouldn't take up such a big challenge of sculpting a Durga, but even then, he left his bed early one morning and started work on the basic structure, as if in a trance. After a while when he regained his thoughts, he felt surprised at himself. Who had delegated him this task, he wondered.

Bangshi's wife Janki never opposed any of her husband's actions. After all he was a good man. He was not ill tempered, and was quite fond of his children. Still why did he, for no reason, allow himself to be beaten by others? Bangshi never cried, but there were tears hidden deep in Janki's heart. Each time Bangshi returned with a bloody face after an attack on him, she wept miserably, Each time she feared that he would die!

After making an idol, Bangshi called out to his his wife repeatedly and showed it to her. He had no other friend, there weren't too may visitors to his house either, and if anyone ever did visit, the images would be kept hidden in the room at the back. His wife and his children were the only spectators of his works of art. Janaki found these idols to be quite nice. She bent down in obeisance, touching her head on the floor, but her heart shook from some unknown fear. After all, these gods and goddesses belonged to the upper class, how could they befit a house like her's?

Of late, Bangshi seemed to have lost interest in his main work. The few straw and bamboo baskets and platters that he somehow managed to finish, were sold at the market in Manglahat. Of course that didn't provide enough for running his household. But if anybody ever reminded him of that, he would remain silent, with a fixed look in his eyes. That is why Janaki had started doing this work on her own, she had begun to teach her son also. Their daughter was five years old now, and their son who was nine, was studying in class three.

At times, Bangshi would call his son and ask him, "Don't the boys in your class beat you?" The boy would shake his head vehemently. Was he really speaking the truth or did he not want his father to know? Or was it because he was going dressed in shirts and shoes that the boys from higher castes didn't consider him all that lowly? Had times changed so drastically then?

Apart from the two statuettes of Saraswati, Bangshi didn't preserve any other image. Where did he have so much space, anyway? The Kali idol that he had built was quite huge. After having washed off the clay coating from the top, he would now re-use the frame. He had made the falchion out of some tin sheet, he had preserved that also.

The image of Durga couldn't be too small either, there was the Mother Durga with *Asur*, the demon, and the lion under her feet. All this had to be jointly made. It wasn't possible for Bangshi to make such a large image in his own thatched hut, so he set up a tarpaulin in his courtyard. This tattered tarpaulin had earlier belonged to a shopkeeper in the market, and it was just when that man was about to discard the tarpaulin that Bangshi had asked for it. The man had immediately asked a price of five rupees, but finally settled on three. Bangshi had patched it up and made it somehow fit for use.

Within a few days, Bangshi realized that he would have to accept defeat now. It was not possible for him to make an idol of Durga all by himself. He had only dared to make possible the impossible.

He had never seen a lion, only once when he was a child, he had gone to see two tigers that had been caught in a forest nearby. He had never had the opportunity to see an image of Durga from very close quarters either. Every year, a Durga Puja was held in the zamindar's house, but he was not allowed to enter the pandal. There was a picture of the Durga Ma in the illustrated version of the *Ramayana*, which showed Ramchandra worshipping the Durga before the *Setubandhan*. There was yet another picture in a calendar that hung in the grocery shop. In fact, that one was even larger, Bangshi had often seen it while standing outside the shop.

As days passed by, Bangshi felt more and more disappointed.

No, he just couldn't make it. He would have to give up this idea. For almost a week, he refrained from doing anything on that project. He just lay down and thought.

Unless someone taught him the art of creating this particular image, how would he be able to make it? Did Mushirul Chacha know how to sculpt a Durga? Besides, this work involved a lot of expenditure, and a large amount of paint. Actually, he didn't have to spend much while carving the Kali idol, he had only dissolved some soot from the kerosense lantern in water and mixed it with only a little blue paint. But the Durga had to be painted yellow, the *Asur* in blue, and the lion was to be in a mixed shade of yellow and brown. Besides all these, one needed to paint Durga's robes also, which had not been necessary in sculpting the naked figure of Kali.

Bangshi had almost decided not to waste any more effort on this, rather he was planning to break up the basic frame and put his mind back again on his earlier work, when the very next day, he got into a bus that was leaving for Kailashnagar. This was once again a strange incident. Even while a part of the human mind accepts defeat, the other part possibly wants to remain undefeated.

Bangshi had not stepped out of Kumarnagar much, he didn't need to anyway. After all, everything that he needed was confined to what was available in this small village. He didn't have any specific work in Kailashnagar, but he had heard that there were some families of potters who lived there, and who made various kinds of idols.

After getting down from the bus, Bangshi bought himself 100 gms. of *batashas* and a packet of *Muri* to stave off hunger, and moved around the town in search of those craftsmen. After some time he landed in the potters' locality.

The Durga Pujas were still three months away, but the Durga images were already being made. It had rained heavily last night, the road was steeped in wet mud. Under a thatched roof nearby, Bangshi saw a few potters at work. The room was dark, possibly that is why a lamp had to be lit even during the daytime.

One could stand outside and watch these men work, without anybody protesting. In fact the potters even answered a few queries from the spectators. Of course, Bangshi knew that he was not one of their competitors, he would never sell any of his crafted sculpture again.

He could now see where he had been making errors. The ten hands of the Durga actually posed the main problem. Bangshi had tried to make each arm separately and then join it with the main body, that is why they had been falling off repeatedly. He found that these people had wound some wire with the straw and made the arms along with the frame. After that, they were coated with clay. There was one more problem. The image of Durga was to rest on the lion's back, but wouldn't the lion break under the weight of that huge frame? He noticed that these people had found a special device, the Durga's feet was not actually touching the lion's back, there was about a one inch gap in-between which could be camouflaged by just a coating of clay.

Also, he even noticed the lion very carefully. He moved around and observed each of the images that were being made. Their faces were definitely different. A lion's body was shaped differently from a tiger's. Did a lion really have such a narrow waist? It didn't look proportionate to the rest its body.

One of the Durga statues was almost finished. It was to be sent quite far. A Bengali club in distant Kohima had ordered it. The main image had been completed, only *Kartik* and *Ganesh* remained to be made. The hair too was yet to be plastered. Ma Durga's head was still bald, though her face had already been painted.

Bangshi came closer and asked an aged craftsman, "*Bhaidada*, what makes the statue's face glow so? Do you mix something else with paint?"

The old man said, "Can only paint do? Unless one uses some varnish, this glow cannot be effected. It should be smeared on the face once and then again, after a few days.

Bangshi had never heard of 'varnish'. It was surely available in the market here. After making a few necessary purchases, Bangshi returned home by the last bus, having spent his entire savings!

Once again, he started making idols with a renewed endeavor. This was going to be the last time. After making this ten-armed goddess, he wouldn't need to prove anything more to himself.

Working by night usually meant burning up a lot of kerosene, but Bangshi preferred the very late hours. Of course he had to do the eyes and face during the day, the remaining not-so-delicate parts could be easily done at night, in the light of a small oil lamp.

It was a silent night. The statue of the Goddess had been completed, only the decorations remained to be done. Bangshi continued to stare at his own creation, it was as if he could see an unworldly goddess in front of him. Suddenly, he lowered his voice and said, "Mother, am I a Hindu? Are you my God too? Then why do the *Babus* prevent us from coming close to you? And if we do not have the right to worship you, then why did you bloom so beautifully from just a pulp of mud in my hands alone?"

He stepped outside and lit a *bidi*. It was possibly a full moon tonight, or it might have been so yesterday, the sky was bathed in sparkling light. As he looked up, he felt a stir in his heart. It was a tingling of joy. Yes, he had made it, he had finally achieved what he had wanted. His father, grandfather and the rest of his clan had lived only to meet their needs. But this success of his was of no use. Rather, he had spent much of his hard earned money on it! Once the image was completed, he would undo it little by little. But before that, if he along with his wife and children bowed before the Goddess, then wouldn't that itself be a worship? Would the Mother not accept that act as an offering?

Bangshi's body felt tired, but still he didn't go to bed. He kept standing alone, his body bathed in the silvery moonlight.

After that, like history repeating itself, something happened. Just like that earlier incident in Mushirul's house, some neighbours and relatives, who loved to harm innocent people knowing fully well that they wouldn't in any way benefit from it, went and complained to Narottam and his association about Bangshi's secret work of art. What kind of an abominable practice was going on with the gods and goddesses in a sweepers' locality, they protested? And that too with Ma Durga! Wouldn't it spell doom for everybody!

This time Narottam came charging with an even bigger group.

As they marched towards the house, someone said, "Has that Bangshi lost his head? Does he not learn a lesson even after being beaten so severely?"

"Lost his head – what rubbish! This is sheer wickedness. These low caste people are now wanting to be indulged. They want to desecrate even our religion! Someone must have surely instigated him!"

Bangshi was amazed to see the raiders who stormed in. He folded his hands and said – "Babu, please tell me what was my fault? I didn't make these statues for selling in the market."

"If you don't want to sell them, then why did you make them?"

"Just like that".

"What does that mean –'just like that'?"

Bangshi kept silent. Even he himself didn't know what those words meant, how would he be able to explain it to others?

Narottam said, "I am sure you were planning to worship that image. You low-caste men want to compete with us and start worshipping our God?

"No Babu, its not that. Believe me, please."

But Narottama and his men had not come to argue with Bangshi, they had come to punish him.

Then started the assault. They beat Bangshi till he fell on his face on the ground. His wife came running from inside, his children wailed out in fear. A few others belonging to the sweepers' locality stood a little distance away, totally dazed at the sudden incident.

Narottam wielded his cane angrily and began to destroy the idol.

Someone said, "What are you doing *Dada*? You are destroying the statue of the Mother?"

"Shouldn't I! Should I just leave it and go away?" Narottama retorted. "These sweepers will surely worship it. How can the idol be referred as 'the Mother? It is only a clay statue now. How can it be idolized as a Mother before being infused with a soul through the night mantras?

Anyway, Bangshi's heart must have been like a cat's, that is why he didn't die even after being beaten so hard!

Out of all the heated and noisy words, Narottma's last remark aroused a new realization in Bangshi's mind. A clay statue! However beautifully one made it or decorated it, it would remain just a clay statue. Unless one infused life into it by chanting the right mantras, that idol couldn't become a Goddess or a Mother! That must have been why the Saraswati and the Durga idols had not responded to Bangshi's queries. Bangshi had never seen a priest chant mantras and infuse life into an idol.

After this incident, a group of gentlemen had come once more to this worn-out house in the slum. But that was for a different reason.

Four

Zamindar Abanibhushan Chattopadhyay didn't have much of his *zamindary* left. The pond that lay within the estate was called *Taal Pukur* only by name, actually it wasn't deep enough to drown even a pitcher. People still looked at it with respect from a distance. But to the owner of the house, it was only a growing burden. It was crumbling here and there, and Abanibhushan didn't even have enough money to repair it.

But still, as the zamindar of the land, Abanibhushan tried to keep up a show. None of his three sons lived in Kumaranagar any more. One of them was in Agartala, and the other two in Calcutta. It didn't seem that they would come back here again. Abanibhushan was almost seventy years old now, his youngest son often requested his parents to come and live in Calcutta, but Abanibhushan didn't quite agree to the idea. Who would recognize him in Calcutta? People of unknown and lower castes would brush him aside on the road! He had never liked Calcutta really. At least people in this village still respected him as the young lord, and nobody dared to stand up against him. These were, after all, the only joy and satisfaction in his old age!

After losing his real estate business, Abanibhushan had started a new venture. He had opened up a new company called Binapani Transport Service, named after his wife. There were two buses which shuttled from Kumarnagar to Kailashnagar. But of late, the number of passengers had reduced substantially due to the menace created by the terrorists. Unless it was very necessary, people felt scared to leave their homes and travel long distances. Only a month and a half back, terrorists had forced nine passengers off the bus and shot them dead. They had even tried to set the bus on fire.

The Adivasis from the hills and the forests had been deprived and tortured for too long, they hadn't received most of the advantages and facilities as citizens of the nation. That is why they had now risen in rage, with a weapon in their hand. This uprising was being noticed not only in Tripura, but in many other places in the country. All protests are usually marked by an excessiveness in the beginning. Some irrelevant, illogical events also occur. In fact, they don't hesitate to even kill a few people out of sheer anger. And sometimes even the wrong people get killed!

Abanibhushan's earnings from the bus company had reduced, yet there were some fixed expenditures that had to be met. There was a temple within the compound, where a daily worship was held for over three generations now. Of course, as far as the school was concerned, Abanibhushan had already donated it.

There were only two employees in the office. The rent controller Narottam Samanta's financial condition was much better than Abanibhushan's. He had already removed several acres of land from the estate under a fictitious name, but still hadn't given up his job. After all the name 'rent collector' had its own importance, didn't it?

Abanibhushan had to spend heavily during the Pujas. Only one Puja was held in the entire town of Kumarnagar, and that was within the boundary of the zamindar's estate. A feast was held on the eighth day of the Pujas, and about three hundred people participated in it. One of the main problems of performing a Durga Puja was that once the practice was initiated, it couldn't be stopped. If it was ever discontinued, then the family would apparently be burdened with a curse. Besides, the Puja lasted for four continuous days also.

This year it had been raining continuously throughout the month of Ashwin. It hadn't rained enough at the beginning of the monsoons, and, now with the end approaching, it poured heavily.

Every year, an idol was brought all the way from Kailashnagar. One day, a terribly unfortunate news reached the people of Kumarnagar. A truck carrying an idol for this village had overturned on its way, and even though the driver had survived, his companion had died. Finally, the truck could somehow be hauled from within the waters but by then the idol was only a skeleton of straw.

On hearing the news, Abanibhushan had felt a kind of suppressed joy. Thank God, he wouldn't have to perform any Puja this time. In fact he could even use this opportunity to stall the tradition for ever! But on the face of it, he put up an appearance of a grief struck man.

On hearing the news, Abanibhushan's wife, Binapani wept her heart out. Would there really be no Pujas performed this year! What a destructive proposition this was! What if it brought a curse on her grandchildren, no matter where they were! No, the Pujas couldn't be stalled at any cost. Even Abanibhushan's widowed sister who lived in this house shared the same opinion.

Nowadays, even if men had a kind of superficial faith in religion, they did not give it any importance. It benefited a person to talk of religious faith in many circumstances, one could earn votes easily, and the class and caste discrimination could also be maintained. That is why one had to pretend to be god fearing. But, unlike men, many women still nourished a very strong and genuine religious belief. And this belief gave rise to a number of deep rooted superstitions. Indeed, that explained the reason for Binapani's fear!

So a man was again sent to Kailashnagar to fetch a new idol, but he returned empty handed. Unlike the Saraswati and Lakshmi idols, a Durga statue was never kept for sale throughout the year. They were made strictly as per the number of orders received. The Pujas were just eleven days away. Even the idols which were being prepared as per pre-placed order weren't complete yet, so it wasn't possible to take any further orders now.

That of course ended matters. How could one perform a worship without an idol? Maybe the Mother Goddess herself didn't want her puja be held amidst such heavy rains and scarcity. Alright then, let it remain stalled this time, Abanibhushan breathed a sigh of relief.

There were many in Kumarnagar who on hearing the news felt disappointed, hurt and agitated. There were so many places where not only one, but two or three Pujas were being organized! Actually, the Durga Puja was indeed the main Puja among the other Pujas. Everybody waited eagerly for it. What right did Abanibhushan have to disappoint everyone? Besides what would people living in other cities say? Didn't Kumarnagar have a prestige of its own?

So, a group of representatives, consisting of distinguished people of the town went to discuss the matter with Abanibhushan. After seating them in his living room, Abanibhushan repeatedly told them that he had no wish to stall the Puja celebrations, after all this had been his family Puja from over generations. Of course, nobody knew what would happen after his death, but till he lived, he would like to continue the tradition even through difficult times. However, no Durga idol was available now. One instalment of money for buying an idol had already gone down the drain. Nevertheless, he was prepared to get another idol if possible.

Someone from within the group of representatives suddenly said – "There is someone here in Kumarnagar who can make such images."

There was a complete silence for a few seconds. Everybody knew the man being referred to, but nobody mentioned his name.

After a while, Narottama said, "Has our country reached such an unfortunate state that we must live to see a bearer become a king, a barber become a doctor, a cockroach – see a bird, and, and ... a scavenger's son sculpt Goddess Durga?

"Well, that could definitely happen. If a cobbler's son can become a president, then ..." Priyanath Babu, the postmaster added.

Something had happened in the meantime. Many local people had not been able to accept the earlier assault on Bangshi. Its not that everybody belonging to the upper class had a bad heart. There were some among them who gave indulgence or support to wrong and unjust causes. But there were also many others from the same class who protested against such injustice. The village postmaster, the Head Master, the history teacher, a couple of doctors and a few students didn't follow any class or caste discrimination. There was yet another group of leftists. This group had conspired against Narottam. In fact the incident had been discussed in many places.

But this refusal to accept and an active effort to counteract such social evils didn't always go hand in hand. It was only a few days back, when a woman from Taroidi, a village just twelve kilometers from here, was declared a witch and burnt to death. Many had shuddered at the news, none of them had such superstitious of believing in witches even in this modern age. But had even a single group of people gone there for any redressal? That somehow had never happened, only a sense of sad unfulfillment remained in their heart. Even the police visited such areas seven or ten days later, just for the sake of it.

All of a sudden now, a few men burst out in a loud protest.

Priyanath again said, "Narottam Babu, you had really committed on offence by assaulting Bangshi. It could have even turned into a police case."

"Are you trying to threaten me?" Narottama shouted back.

"Who will lodge the police case ... you? Why didn't you? You are quite chummy with the police, aren't you?"

"No, that's not the issue." Priyanath replied. "What I am saying is that morally."

"Oh keep your morality to yourself, sir. I was not the only one present there. Such incidents are harmful for the society, and the police do not bother with such things." Narottam retorted.

"I have heard that you had beaten him earlier also." Priyanath said. "Who has given you the charge of looking after the society! And why should others obey your dictates anyway?"

Narottam said, "It doesn't really matter whether you listen to me or not. That man is a thief, he is a scoundrel. He had even entered the temple once to steal, and now he is trying to destroy our religion! Should we still just stand and watch him do that? Why don't you ask the Zamindar what that boy had done."

Vishnupada, the headmaster now intervened. "Why are you getting so agitated? Instead, why don't all of you get together and see how the Pujas can be held. When that boy can make idols, what is the harm in asking him to make one for us? When an image is brought from some other place, does anybody bother about the social identity of the man who made it?"

Narottam continued to protest. "But does that mean that we should watch someone who is nothing but a low caste swindler and cheat make a holy image for us? Wouldn't that be a sacrilege? If after this, a sweeper wishes to marry your daughter, will you agree?"

Vishnupada didn't know how to answer such an odd question.

Priyanath tried to divert a bit. He said, "Wasn't it you Narottam who had once said that until the soul is implanted into the clay statue through various religious chants, the statue does not get transformed to Mother Durga. Remember, even a low caste man can lay his hands on mud and clay, so what is the harm if he moulds a statue with that?"

Narottama grimaced and said, "I don't want to argue any further with you."

Priyanath wouldn't listen still. He said, "Do you know who stitches the traditional dress that you adorn the Goddess with? It's the Muslims. Its they who stitch these clothes in Calcutta, I have seen it with my own eyes. The crown on Ma Durga's head is also designed by Muslim craftsmen!"

"You seem to be greatly in love with Muslims, isn't it? By the way, where did you live earlier? They must have driven you here from the other side of the Bengal border, didn't they!"

"Whatever it is, we are definitely going to celebrate the Pujas this time!" A young voice shouted from somewhere at the back.

Abanibhushan hadn't spoken for long. Suddenly he flared up and said, "Who are you to dictate whether a puja should or should not be held in my house! Any away, this is my last word – no idol made by a scavenger's son will ever enter the boundaries of my house! Never, ever! You may however see if you can get hold of an idol from somewhere else."

People fell silent again.

Abanibhushan shook with anger. As he tried to control his temper, he kept thinking of his wife Binapani. How was he going to pacify her? She didn't want to listen to any reasoning.

She had even suggested selling off her ornaments to get the Pujas started!

"Then why don't we have only a symbolic ritual, and worship an urn instead." Vishnupada suggested. "But even that would have to be as per the *shastras.*"

Priyanath said – "But without an idol, the worship doesn't quite feel complete. The young children –"

Abanibhushan looked up and replied in a rather calm voice this time. "There is another way out. Why don't the boys from the Tarun Sangha club start celebrating the annual Durga Puja on the lawn in front of my house. If they can raise some funds this year, then its well and good, otherwise I will bear the major cost for the first year. But only the members of my family will be given the right to be the first to participate in a separate offering ceremony every day. I will not be bothered with where they get the idol from."

A joyous cry filled the room.

Vishnupada said, "Chatterjee Sir, you have really come up with a wonderful suggestion."

Narottaam turned an appreciative glance towards his master. The old man could still think so well! Indeed, it would be like killing a snake and yet not breaking the stick. The Pujas would be held, but not inside the house. He wouldn't have to suffer the insult of bringing inside the house, an image prepared by that low-caste boy who he had once assaulted.

The boys from the Tarun Sangha jumped at the proposal.

Another club by the name of *Sabuj Sangha* located in some other locality usually celebrated the Kali Puja. But it was being heard from some reliable source, that they would be starting the Durga Puja from this year as well. And should the Tarun Sangha just sit and do nothing?

First of all, they would have to settle matters regarding the image of the Goddess.

So, a group of ten boys left for Bangshi's house.

What was Bangshi's condition now? In spite of that severe beating, he hadn't broken a leg or arm, but this time the attack had left him completely broken in spirit. He no longer felt inspired to engage in any kind of creative work. Even his eyes seemed to have lost their shine. Earlier, he used to sit in front of a small mirror in the verandah and shave twice a week. But now he had given up shaving altogether. There was a stubble on his chin. He spent most of his time, making only cane baskets. He had stopped working with bamboo altogether, confining only to cane products. He had even stopped going to the market for the last three weeks and sent his wife and son instead. The heavy monsoon rains had taken their toll, the thatched roof of his house now hung low on one side, but he didn't feel any urge to prop up the bamboo pole which supported it.

At times Bangshi would stare at his own hands and observe his fingers very carefully. Did he have leprosy? Why had it not attacked him as yet, he wondered. In that case he would get to know everything. After all, if God's curse came true, it wouldn't be possible to fight it!

On hearing footsteps outside, and his own name being called out, Bangshi came and stood at the front door.

One of the men, a representative of the Tarun Sangha Club came forward and said "Listen Bangshi, there's good news for you. You will have to build an image of Ma Durga again and it will be worshipped in the Pujas. We will arrange it."

Bangshi kept staring at the man blankly as if he couldn't understand anything.

The man repeated. "You'll have to make a Durga idol again and there's not much time left really."

This time Bangshi spoke slowly, "I will not be able to do it Sir."

"Why not? You'll get all the money that you need."

"Babu, I don't have that capability any more. I've lost all my strength."

"You can't afford to say that now. There's hardly any time left. I will send you two very helpful workers. They'll help with you everything. I'll also get you some medicines from the doctor."

"Believe me Sir, I really can't do it. You may beat me if you wish."

Suddenly there was an uproar. The club representative who had spoken earlier said, "Who will dare to beat you? If anyone ever again ... if anyone ever lays a hand on you, we will deal with him appropriately."

But Bangshi still shook his head.

At this time, Vishnupada stepped forward and placed a comforting hand on Bangshi's back. "Why are you behaving like this, son? why don't you agree?" He asked.

Someone else from the crowd joined in, "You know, people would despise us if our Puja gets stalled. You know Bangshi, the honour and dignity of Kumarnagar depends totally on you now."

The man whom no one had bothered about in all these years, the one whose existence had meant nothing to others it was the same person on who they were now trying to rest the responsibility of upholding the dignity and honour of their city! What an irony!

Without paying any heed to the man's words, Bangshi turned to Vishnupada. "Babu, did you place your hand on my back just now?"

"Why do you ask me that? Don't you like being touched?"

"But we're untouchables. People from the upper castes need to wash themselves if they ever touch us."

Priyanath quipped in with a hint of humour, "Oh in that case, The Headmaster may take a dip in the waters on his way back."

Vishnupada said, "I don't believe in all that. You might be unclean when you are cleaning garbage and working as a sweeper. But why should I not touch you at other times?"

"But hadn't you told me earlier that it's a sin for me to make idols, and that if I make one, it cannot be worshipped as a God!"

"No, we had never said anything like that. In fact we had pulled up that rascal Narottam for what he did to you. He will not dare to utter a sound again."

"Then is it not true that the image loses its sanctity if I touch it?"

At this point, an elderly man intervened. "Come on, let's not talk about all that now. Once the image is taken to the *pandal*, and a few drops of Ganga water sprinkled on its head with sacred chants, it can regain its sanctity."

Turning towards that gentleman, Bangshi spoke in a very soft and feeble voice – "Babu, why cant you sprinkle a few drops of Ganga water on my head and make me pure? If a clay doll can gain sanctity, why can't human beings also? Will I have to remain a low caste all my life?"

The old man tried to explain. "It's your birth in a lowly family that is at fault. What can you do about it? You must have committed a sin in your previous birth. That is why you have been born in a low caste family. Try and follow the virtuous path in this life and you will definitely be born a gentleman in the next."

"Rubbish." An angry young man protested. "What is all this about previous and next birth? Isn't it the people from the higher castes who commit the most sins? Gandhiji had said that all these people like Bangshi are *Harijans* and that all men are equal."

"Hah, Gandhiji!" Priyanath muttered to himself. It's so long since he died, is there anything left of him now!*Harijan* indeed! By giving them such an ostentatious name, he has only kept them away from mainstream society. Why, he never struck at the root of all this class-distinction. The word *Harijan* necessarily implied a *Chamar* or *Chandal*. Will they ever be raised to the status of the Ghoshes, Boses, the Mitras or the Chatterjees and Gangulys? Even today, the *Harijans* are being burnt down for daring to drink water from the same well as the caste Hindus."

Of course Priyanath was only talking to himself. After all, he was a government employee, How could he express his opinions publicly? He hadn't requested Bangshi even once.

But the rest of them were talking in such loud and agitated voices that Bangshi's words remained unheard. They kept on making promises, one after another. Yes, they would buy him all the things needed for making the idol, which included a silk robe for Ma Durga, the material for her hair, the traditional dress, paints, the sequined necklace and everything else. Of course, Bangshi would also be paid an advance money for the job They would send him two assistants. In fact, the secretary of the club even announced that the MLA would come to inaugurate the Puja on the first day, and that Bangshi himself would be made the chief guest.

After all this, Bangshi had no other option but to agree.

For the next few days the word "*Harijan*" created a lot of stir among the public. The word was quite in vogue in big cities and in newspapers, but was not used commonly in such small *muffasals* yet. Actually, the *Harijans* themselves didn't know that they were *Harijans!*

Using this as a pretext, many others pretended to be progressive. Since they had agreed to have a *Harijan* make the image, then why not spread the glory of the *Harijans*. It could even create an example for the other states. In case the MLA failed to turn up finally, why not have the festival inaugurated by a *Harijan* like Bangshi himself, they suggested.

In the midst of this, the priest posed a rather unexpected problem.

After the earlier priest had been driven away, there had been no other priest for the last six months. Abanibhushan himself had to perform the rituals. A new priest had been brought from Udaipur. He was an extremely aged man of feeble health, and had no family. In fact, he couldn't have found a job anywhere else. Actually, he was a helpless man, but he was spirited. He was rather gruff in his speech, not allowing any compromise or laxity in the rituals. Besides, people always showed greater respect for priests and monks of a harsh temperament. They considered their harshness as a proof of their dedication. At times, this priest, Sasanka Bhattacharjee did not spare even the Zamindar's wife for committing the slightest errors in ritualistic practices.

Right from the start, Sasanka Bhattacharjee had been totally opposed to the idea of a sweeper's son making the image of the Goddess. He was against worshipping that image. But where could one find another priest? The boys from the club tried to intimidate him indirectly. And finally he agreed to their demand on one condition. Would that sweeper's son visit the puja pandal also? Wouldn't that be drawing other low caste people to the puja pandal? No this just couldn't be allowed, the scriptures had forbidden chanting religious mantras in the presence of low caste and the downtrodden in society. So they would have to be prevented from entering the *pandal*, only then Sasanka Bhattacharya would agree to sound the puja bell.

Immediately, a hushed whisper started among the people. Could Bangshi be forbidden to come? Besides, he had already been promised that he would be made the chief guest.

Some of the members were already losing their interest, they had heard from their parents that the matter was being stretched too far. Many Brahmins and Kayasthas would not come if the sweepers and other lower castes also visited the *pandal*. Such rumours were already rampant.

If people did not come, what was the significance of carrying out the puja with such pomp and show? It was for this alone that many refused to give any donation. Pradip, who was the secretary of the Tarun Sangha, had been nicknamed 'manage master' by his friends. True to his name, he now set out for Bangshi's house to see if he could explain matters.

The MLA had already informed that he wouldn't be able to come, so what was the use of having the inaugural function? It might as well be cancelled. Next year a few artists could be invited and the show could be carried out on a grand scale.

On meeting Bangshi, Pradip said, "See, the inaugural function has been cancelled. We will come and take you on the Vijaya *Dashami* day, and you'll be given a felicitation. You don't have to go on any of the earlier three days. We'll keep a surprise for everybody on the *Dashami* day. Besides, some people are going to offer sacrifices and take vows on those days, so why bother to go then? You will be asked to make the image next year too, on a much larger scale, and you'll be cutting the inaugural ribbon on the *Sasthi* day also."

Bangshi was engaged in his work, he didn't have time to pay any importance to such words. Only once he said, "You want that I shouldn't go, is it? Alright then, I will not."

By the *Panchami* evening, the Durga idol arrived at the pandal that had just been erected on the lawn facing the zamindar's house. But before that, Vishnupada and a few others had come to inspect it. It had not been possible to make the other accompanying images namely those of the Lakshmi, Saraswati, Kartik and Ganesh within such a short time. And in any case these gods and goddesses would be soon worshipped individually within a period of three months from each other. The statue of the Mother Durga with her ten arms, riding a lion was enough. Vishnupada and the others felt enchanted by what they saw.

"Wonderful, this is even better than the one made by the artists in Kailashnagar." They said, in a tone of appreciation.

It was mainly out of Vishnupada's excessive eagerness that the artist's name got inscribed on the dais on which the image was placed. The words "Bangshidhari Harijan" shone in bold letters. After all, the name of the sculptor was always found at the feet of every idol.

Even though the inaugural function had been cancelled, the ceremonial awakening of the Goddess Durga on the morning of the sixth day was definitely going to be held. Many honoured guests and important people arrived at the pandal. Abanibhushan sat on a chair, and his wife Binapani sat with the other ladies, arranging the articles needed for the religious ceremony.

The idol seemed to have a little too much hair on her head. One of its eyes was hidden under a few strands. As soon as the priest moved them aside to decorate the Goddess's forehead with sandalwood paste, he was completely taken aback.

"What is this?" He said, startled." Am I to welcome a one eyed Goddess?"

Everybody was shocked to see that the goddess had only one-eye. That eye looked perfect, but the other one had no pupil, it was painted completely white.

How could this have happened? Had Bangshi forgotten to draw the other eye? The way he had to hurry through this work, it was quite possible for him to have made such a mistake. Or maybe it was just plain mischief on his part!

Anyway, what could they do now? Couldn't someone in this city draw the other eye? Nobody volunteered. A young boy who studied in Class nine at the Government school, and who lived close by, was known to draw and sketch on paper. The organizers of the Puja committee contacted him and had him brought over. The boy stood trembling in fear. Was it all that easy to draw Ma Durga's eyes? What if the two eyes turned out differently! Besides he was used to sketching with a pencil or a pen, and was not trained in the use of paint and brush!

The boy could not be forced. It would be even more ominous if the eyes looked crooked! If even a goat which was to be sacrificed on the Durga Puja day, had to be completely free from any blemish, then how could the Goddess herself afford to have such imperfection?

So they had no other option but to call Bangshi.

" Is that lad going to come here?" Sasanka Bhattacharya asked in a dry voice.

This time, Abanibhushan flared up. He could no longer contain his patience. "Listen Pandit," He said. "Don't try to cross your limits! Did you think that this huge idol would be carried all the way to that slum? When we had to accept all this, how much more unsanctified could this place get just from his visit?"

A few volunteers rushed off, and returned holding Bangshi by the arms. Anticipating that their father was about to be assaulted again, Bangshi's children also followed him.

Everybody made way, and Bangshi was made to stand on the ground, a little away from the idol.

"What is this, Bangshi?" Bishnupada asked. "Did you really forget to draw one eye of the Goddess?"

Bangshi kept standing silently, as if he could not even

remember whether he had really forgotten to paint the eye or not.

Priyanath turned to Bishnupada and whispered, "In a way, the right thing has happened. After all, these Gods and goddesses are all very partial. They are not kind towards the poor at all, are they?"

One just couldn't bear to look at the Durga's face now. How could the absence of just one eye make such an otherwise beautiful face look so ugly?

The place at the bottom of the dias where Bangshi's name had been inscribed, had been covered with a sticker.

Bangshi threw a quick glance in that direction, and then moved closer to the idol with a pot of paint and brush in his hand. At first, he stood still for a few moments with his eyes closed, as if he was meditating, even though he didn't know any chants.

After a while he opened his eyes and with a swift stroke of the brush, painted the icon's eyebrow, just like the other one. Then he drew the outline for the eye. Painting the eyeball took somewhat more time. In the end, he concentrated on the very delicate eyelashes.

Everybody clapped in appreciation.

Tearing off the plaster that was stuck over his name, Bangshi came back to his earlier place. Then joining his hands together very politely, he said, "Sirs, please forgive me if I have made any mistakes."

Seeing the only blemish on the otherwise perfectly sculptured idol vanish, people had already forgiven him. "No, don't say that, you have really done a very god job." They said.

Bangshi's daughter lowered her voice and said – "Baba, see, it seems as if Mother Durga is looking directly at us."

Abanibhushan called the priest and said, "Come on Pandit, start the Puja now. Why delay any more? "

Gesturing through his eyes at Bangshi, Sasanka asked, "Is he going to remain here even now?"

A young doctor from the crowdimmediately stood up and said –"Yes, he is. Everybody is welcome to a public puja. You have been making too many demands right from the start. If you don't want to perform the rituals, then please move off. I am also a Brahim's son. I can read out the chants."

Sasanka Bhattacharya let out a deep sigh. One who had known poverty as a daily companion, couldn't afford to be stubborn After all, it was during the days of the Puja when he earned the maximum.

Still, he said sarcastically – "So, after this, should we expect even the Muslims to attend this event?"

"Yes they will. If any of them wishes to, he can come. Don't we too go to visit the Pir Sahab's tomb?"

Bangshi looked up and said, "My teacher was Sheikh Mushirul Rehman. It was he who had taught me to sculpt statues."

Then, touching his forehead with folded hands, he bowed in reverence. It wasn't clear whether Bangshi's salute was directed towards the Goddess or towards his own teacher. But when he lowered his hands, tears were seen streaming down his eyes.

Glossary

ajan	an official call to Muslims to attend prayer meting in a mosque
amma	mother
arati	an act of greeting an Deity with a light, flowers etc.
arre	term used in addressing or hailing
asur	a demon
babu	a respectful title or term for addressing a gentleman
bansh	bamboo
barda	elder brother
batasha	a light sweet made of sugar or molasses
bel	a kind of flower
bhindi	a vegetable-lady's finger
bidis	a kind of slender cigarette rolled in a tree leaf
bijuri	lightning
boudi	elder brother's wife
chacha	uncle
chadar	shawl
chamar	a shoemaker by caste
chanachur	crisp snack prepared by frying chick peas and other ingredients with

GLOSSARY

chandal	one of the lowest castes among Hindus
chatu	flour made of barley, maize etc.
chulla	an oven, furnace
dada	elder brother
dal	soup of pigeon pea
dhoti and kurta	Indian dress for men
dulabhai	sister's husband
fakir	a mendicant ascetic
ganja	Indian hemp
garud	name of the prince of birds on whom Lord Vishnu rides
gherao	surrounded, besieged
gur	molasses
huzoor	a term for addressing a master, or an honorable person
kajia	a fight
kali	an Indian Goddess
karabi	oleander flower
khaini	a quid of tobacco
luchis	kind of small and thin saucer shaped bread fried in ghee.
mahakurma	
moong daal	soup of pigeon-pea
muri	a kind of light eatable made by parching rice on hot sand
namaste	a manner of greeting

namaz	the Muslim system of saying one's prayer.
paneer	cheese
panta bhat	rice cooked overnight and kept steeped in water.
pantar ghugnee	a snack made out of minced mutton and peas
pishima	father's sister
pranam	act of showing respect by bending down and touching one's feet
rajdhani	The capital of a country or state
ram ram	an expression of a salutation in courtesy
roti	a kind of thin circular shaped bread made out of wheat
shanty jal	holy water sprinkled after a religious function, to ward off evil
shastras	scriptures
shuntki maach	seasoned fish
thir	still (poetic use)
ustad	a music trainer, an expert
veena	a stringed musical instrument
zamindar	landlord

CPSIA information can be obtained
at www.ICGtesting.com
Printed in the USA
BVHW032144031122
651146BV00012B/265

9 788188 575831